JOAN BAUER

HOPE WAS HERE

SCHOLASTIC INC.

New York Toronto London Auckland Sydney
Mexico City New Delhi Hong Kong Buenos Aires

ISBN-13: 978-0-439-52348-6
ISBN-10: 0-439-52348-6

12 11 10 9 8 7 6 5 4 3 2   20 21 22 23 24

Printed in the U.S.A.   40

First Scholastic paperback printing, October 2003
Book designed by Gunta Alexander
Text set in Janson

FOR PASTOR JOANN CLARK,
LAURA SMALLEY, AND RITA ZUIDEMA—
MIDWIVES SURE AND TRUE

Somehow I knew my time had come when Bambi Barnes tore her order book into little pieces, hurled it in the air like confetti, and got fired from the Rainbow Diner in Pensacola right in the middle of lunchtime rush. She'd been sobbing by the decaf urn, having accidentally spilled a bowl of navy bean soup in the lap of a man who was, as we say in the restaurant game, one taco short of a combo platter. Gib, the day manager, was screaming at her to stop crying, which made her cry all the more, which led to the firing and her stomping out the door wailing how life wasn't fair, right in front of the hungry customers. That's when Gib turned to me.

"You want her job?"

I was a bus girl at the time, which meant I cleaned off dirty tables and brought people water and silverware. I'd been salivating for years to be a waitress.

I stood up tall. "Yes, I sure do."

"You going to cry on me, fall apart if something goes wrong?"

And I saw right then if you're going to cut the mustard in

food service, you'd better know how to handle turmoil. I straightened my shoulders, did my best to look like flint.

"I'm the toughest female you've ever seen," I assured him.

"You're hired then. Take the counter."

It was my fourteenth birthday, and I took to waitressing like a hungry trucker tackles a T-bone. That job was the biggest birthday present I'd ever gotten, next to getting my name changed legally when I was twelve.

I've had three waitressing jobs over the last two and a half years—slung hash from Pensacola to Brooklyn—made money that most teenagers only dream about. Brooklyn was the best place yet.

And now I've got to leave.

"You ready?" My aunt Addie asked me the question.

We were standing by the boarded-up windows of what had once been the greatest diner in Brooklyn. The Blue Box was shut up like a tomb. You couldn't see the green vinyl booths by the window or the big oval counter that sat in the middle of the place like the center ring in a circus. There weren't any whiffs of stuffed pork tenderloin with apricots or country meatloaf with garlic mashed potatoes or Addie's famous cinnamon ice cream dripping down that deep-dish apple pie of hers with crust so buttery it would bring cabdrivers to their knees in pure reverence. Anyone from Brooklyn knows cabdrivers don't bow the knee for much.

The sign wasn't lit up like it had been for those sweet eighteen months that Addie had been chief cook and part owner with Gleason Beal, Slime Scourge of the Earth.

I stood there remembering how Gleason had stolen the money from the cash register one night; how he'd cleared out the business bank account and headed off for parts unknown with Charlene the night waitress and our money. We'd limped by for a few months on what we made daily, but when the furnace died ($10,000) and the roof started leaking ($4,000) and the monthly bills came due, we were toast. Addie had to close the place down before the bill collectors did.

Bill collectors are like cheap tippers—they always leave bad feelings behind.

I touched the boarded-up window. I'd invented a sandwich here when I was fifteen—the Keep Hoping. It had layers of smoked turkey, sun-dried tomatoes, fresh mozzarella, and chopped salad greens with red wine vinaigrette on a sourdough roll. People ordered it like mad, too, because hope is something that everyone needs. It was a sandwich for our time.

I took out my blue pen and wrote HOPE WAS HERE in tiny letters on one of the boards. Hope is my name. Whenever I leave a place I write this real small someplace significant just to make the statement that I'd been there and made an impact. I've never defaced anything—never carved it into a tree or painted it on a sidewalk or a street sign. I wrote HOPE WAS HERE in half-inch-tall letters above the rotating dessert case at the Ballyhoo Grill back in South Carolina before we moved to New York. It's one of the ways I say good-bye to a place. I've had tons of practice doing that.

"I'm ready," I said.

Addie squared her shoulders. "Let's do it."

We walked across the street to the old Buick that was packed to the hilt with everything we owned and had a U-Haul trailer chained to the back.

It was May 26. We were heading to Mulhoney, Wisconsin, to start work in a diner there that needed a professional manager and cook (Addie), was short on waitresses (me), and was giving us an apartment. The man we were going to work for had been diagnosed with leukemia and needed help fast. I don't mean to sound ungenerous, but working for a close-to-dying man didn't sound like a great career move to me. I had to leave school right before the end of my undistinguished sophomore year, too.

I hate leaving places I love.

We were about to get into the car just as Morty the cab-driver double-parked his Yellow taxi.

Good old Morty. The first time I waited on him, he un-loosened his belt a notch before he even looked at the menu.

I knew I had a true believer.

I raised my hand to a great tipper.

"You always took care of me, kid!" He shouted this from across the street as a UPS truck started honking at him to move his cab.

"I tried, Morty!"

"Wherever you go, you'll do okay. You got heart!"

The UPS driver screamed something heartless at Morty, who screamed back, *Watch your mouth, big man in a brown truck!*

I didn't know what kind of customers I'd get in Wisconsin. Miriam Lahey, one of my two best friends, had given me a NEW YORK FOREVER T-shirt as a good-bye present and said solemnly, "There's a lot of cheese where you're going, Hope. I'm not sure how this affects people long term. Wear this shirt and remember who you are."

Miriam straightened her faux-leopard vest, flipped back the five earrings dangling from her right lobe, and hugged me hard.

We got in the car. Addie started it up. "On to greener pastures," she said and drove the Buick forward. It groaned with the weight of the U-Haul as we headed down Atlantic Avenue, the best place I've ever known in my whole life.

She grabbed my hand and gave it a squeeze.

Addie never promised that life would be easy, but she did promise that if I hung with her the food would be good.

Believe me when I tell you, I know about survival.

I was born too early and much too small (two pounds and five ounces). For the first month of my life I kept gasping for air, like I couldn't get the hang of breathing. I couldn't eat either; couldn't suck a bottle. The doctors didn't think I would make it. Shows what they know. My mother didn't want the responsibility of a baby so she left me with Addie, her older sister, and went off to live her own life. I've seen her exactly three times since I was born—when she visited on my fifth, eighth, and thirteenth birthdays.

Each time she talked about being a waitress. What made a good one ("great hands and personality"). What were the pitfalls ("crazed cooks and being on your feet all day"); what was the biggest tip she ever got ($300 from a plumber who had just won the instant lottery).

Each time she told me, "Hon, leaving you with Addie was

the best thing I could have done for you. You need constants in your life." She had a different hair color each time she said it.

Addie's been my number-one constant. She stood by me in the hospital at my little oxygen tent telling me to come on and get strong. The doctors told her to give up, but giving up isn't Addie's way. She'd wanted a baby all her life, and after three miscarriages and her no-good husband, Malcolm, deserting her for that thin-lipped dental hygienist, I was her last chance at motherhood. So I guess I pulled through because somehow I knew Addie needed me.

Because of this, I don't buy into traditional roles. My favorite book when I was little had pictures of baby animals, like foxes and lambs and ducklings, who were being raised by other animals, like dogs, geese, and wolves.

Addie said it was our story.

But my mom, Deena, left me with two things. One I kept—her gift of waitressing; the other I threw away—the name she gave me at birth, which, I swear, was Tulip.

How a person can look at a two-pound baby all wired up in a hospital box and think *Tulip* is beyond me. On my eighth birthday I asked Mom why she named me that. I remember her laughing and saying she'd seen a movie set in Holland and the actress was running through a bed of tulips as happy as could be.

"I wanted to think of you that way," she cooed in her breathy voice. "Happy and free. Running through tulips."

My good friend Lourdes, who has her own name challenge, said it could have been worse; that movie actress could have been running through a field of poison ivy or snapdragons. It took me twelve years to break free of the curse—kids teasing me, shuddering when the teacher called on me in class. By the time I was fourteen I'd been to six different schools and lived in five states, because although Addie was a great cook, the restaurants she worked for kept going belly-up. I know first-hand about change and adaptability. But Tulip is not a name you adapt to, so on my twelfth birthday Addie let me change it legally. She made me think hard about what I wanted to be called, got a book of names with their definitions that we pored through. And when we came to *Hope*, I knew I'd found it. I think hope is just about the best thing a person can have.

Addie said I had to think doubly hard about a name like Hope because it's a lot to live up to. People expect things from Hopes that they don't expect from Pattys and Lisas and Danielles. People expect Hopes to be cheerful and positive. So I wrote out the name on a three-by-five card and carried it around with me for a month—HOPE YANCEY. At the end of the month Addie asked, "You think you're up to carrying that name?"

I said I was.

"Okay, Hope Yancey, let's make it official."

I got all dressed up, and Addie and I took the bus to the courthouse in downtown St. Louis, where we were living at the time. The clerk who processed my papers at the courthouse said if anyone deserved the name Hope, it was me. I made her hopeful just standing there.

I wasn't feeling too hopeful at the moment.

Addie was flying on the interstate to Wisconsin, the land of lactose.

I stared out the window as the Buick roared west to whatever.

2

We'd been driving for hours. Addie was talking in stressed-out blurts.

"Got to find a sausage wholesaler who knows the power of bratwurst.

"Got to move in fast with the butterscotch cream pie, then introduce the flank steak."

I looked in the backseat of the Buick, piled with the cardboard cartons of my life. When you move a lot, you have a few things you bring with you that have stood the test of time: I've got my Webster's dictionary, because words are important. I've got my Roget's thesaurus, because sometimes finding the right word requires assistance. I've got my Replogle globe, because you've got to keep a world view, you can't just live like you're the only person on the planet who matters. I've got my eleven scrapbooks of most of the places I've lived, complete with photographs and all my significant comments about people, places, and food. Addie says it's easy to go to a new place and feel like you don't have a history, so you have to lug your history around with you or it's too easy to forget.

I'll tell you why I keep my scrapbooks. It's in case my real father shows up. I never met him, don't even know his name. My mother says she doesn't know who he is either. You'd think she'd try to zero in on an important thing like that. But to tell the truth, I'm not sure she's being honest. I've got this feeling that my dad's out there searching for me. When he bursts through the door and tells me he's spent a fortune on detectives who've been looking all over the world for me, I'm not going to sit there like a dumb cluck when he asks me what I've been doing. I'm going to yank out my eleven scrapbooks filled with my experiences and innermost thoughts on life lived in three time zones in America.

I was a Girl Scout for three months when we lived in Atlanta. I couldn't get those square knots down for anything, but I got the big concept.

Be prepared.

Addie always told me, "It's more important to get the big concept than be an expert in the small stuff."

Here's the big concept I was thinking about today. I don't expect life to be easy. It hasn't been yet and I'm not holding out for smooth sailing in the future. Not everyone likes this philosophy, but it makes sense to me because when life hits the skids, I don't have to regroup as much as the people who walk around in a cloud like the world owes them a joyful existence.

Harrison Beckworth-McCoy, my best male friend at school, always said that was the thing he liked most about me. He had given me a good-bye present, and I was opening it now as Addie pushed the Buick through Ohio. Inside the box was a small glass prism that caught the sun. A hand-printed note from Harrison read, "New places always help us look at life differently. I will miss you, but won't lose you."

Harrison was always saying sensitive things like that, which put him instantly on Jocelyn Lindstrom's male sensitivity chart. He was the only male either of us knew who had made the chart consistently over twelve months. Donald Raspigi, who occasionally said sensitive things like "Nice sweater," had been on twice.

Enter memories, sweet and sour.

Harrison and me baking enormous mocha chip cookies for the high school bake sale and having them stolen on the Lexington Avenue subway.

Harrison's African fighting fish, Luther, who ate Chef Boyardee Ravioli without chewing.

Harrison reading my mother's photocopied annual Christmas letter that she sent to family and friends—"Dear Friends..." (She'd cross out "Friends" and write in "Addie and my little Tulip.") Harrison commenting that motherhood should be like driving a car—you should have to pass a test before you get to do it legally.

I held the prism up to the light. The sun hit it and showered colors through the windshield.

"Now isn't that something?" Addie said, smiling at the sight.

"Yeah." I looked out the window, trying not to cry.

We stayed at a Budget Inn; South Bend, Indiana. Crashed late; woke up early. Here I was—my body heading to one place, my heart stuck in another. My mind's got questions and no answers.

What kinds of kids live in Mulhoney, Wisconsin?

Would they like me?

Would I like them?

Have they ever eaten sushi? That's usually how I determine food sophistication.

Maybe a personal ad would get the ball rolling.

Insightful, hardworking 16-year-old girl, emotionally generous and witty, seeks friend/pal/chum to while away meaningful hours. Picky eaters need not reply.

We pushed through to Illinois, Sears Tower shouldering us; caught I-94 up to Wisconsin. Green rolling hills. Cheese billboards. Grazing cows. Basic bovine boredom. WISCONSIN— AMERICA'S DAIRYLAND, proclaimed a sign.

I looked at Addie, her face committed to make it in Cowville. *We're city people!* I wanted to shout. I didn't shout it, though. I felt a hint of the old, bad anger rising up like it used to when I was younger and we had to move. When I was ten I ran away to my friend Lyla's house as Addie was packing the car.

"I'm not going to Atlanta!" I screamed at Addie's back. *"You can't make me!"*

I hit the passenger door of the Buick. That dent is still there today (I was holding a rock at the time). Lyla hid me in her attic with root beer and Fritos, but after a while I got scared thinking that Addie might leave me flat like my mom did.

I ran the two blocks back home.

Addie saw me tearing around the corner; she put the last of the boxes in the U-Haul. "I wouldn't have gone without you."

I wanted to believe that more than anything.

Addie sat down on the curb. I sat next to her. "I'm not sure if you'll understand this," she said. "But I need you as much as you need me. You want to write that down? Keep it in your pocket so you don't forget?"

I looked at the packed-up Buick. "I'll remember."

"There'll be a test later." Addie examined the dent in the door. "We need to get you something else to hit." Then she hugged me with permanence.

West now into Mulhoney, on the outskirts of Milwaukee.

My brain flooded with memories of other new starts.

Eighth grade. Pensacola, Florida. Day one.

I stand on the basketball court and shout, "Look, does anyone here want to be my friend?"

Two kids come forward. That's the power of assertiveness training.

Brooklyn. Soccer practice. St. Edmond's High.

Miriam Lahey and me. She's playing with a ladybug on her shin guard. I've been on the bench so long, I forgot how to play the game. I say, "Do you think athletics is teaching us group dynamics and building our self-esteem?"

Miriam laughs, lifts the ladybug on her finger, transfers it to mine. We've been pals ever since.

I closed my eyes, missing Miriam—even her brief, weird poetry.

> *Perchance, I would listen.*
> *Have you said anything?*

I gave a deep-toned sigh and looked in the file folder that Addie had put together on the new restaurant we were going to work at. It had all her notes about what the place needed and what she'd discussed with the owner. The menu was deep blue. It had a sketch of a two-story frame house. There were double staircases meeting at the front door from the right and the left. The diner was called the Welcome Stairways.

In Brooklyn there were regular stairways.

Addie was maneuvering around a smelly truck. "Read the back of the menu out loud, Hope."

Didn't feel like doing that. Turned the menu over, kept my voice flat.

"From early times, the Quakers had welcome stairways built in front of their homes in Massachusetts. These double stairways descended to the street from the front door and were symbols of Quaker faith and hospitality—constant reminders that all guests were to be welcomed from whichever way they came.

"I can remember running up the welcome stairways at my house as a boy. My mother always said that the stairways symbolized how we must greet whatever changes and difficulties life may bring with firm faith in God." I felt my voice deepen as I said, "Welcome, friend, from whichever way you've come. May God richly bless your journey."

It read "G. T. Stoop, Proprietor" at the end. He was the man with leukemia.

I sat there holding the menu.

The first sign.
WELCOME TO MULHONEY, WISCONSIN, POPULATION 5,492.

The second sign, an arrow pointing left.

WELCOME STAIRWAYS. THIS WAY TO THE BEST DINER IN AMERICA.

Addie sniffed. "Not yet it isn't."

The town was a hodgepodge of styles. We drove past a big dairy that seemed blocks long, past Slick's Barber Shop, where I will *never* get my hair cut. Past the Mulhoney Motor Inn, which had a banner hanging from the second-floor balcony.

REELECT OUR MAYOR—ELI MILLSTONE—THE ONLY MAN FOR MULHONEY.

Left onto Fuller, past the Gospel of Grace Evangelical Center. Two men were fiddling with the engine of an old red van in the parking lot. A small group of African-Americans were watching, wearing blue T-shirts, the letters GOG on the back. A smiling black man in a cool bush hat climbed in the van, revved the motor. The group started clapping, lifting their hands. People got inside. The van headed down the street.

Old brick buildings—red and brown; small houses close together. An Elks Lodge. Addie was catching potholes left and right. At least something reminded me of Brooklyn. A dilapidated building with a faded sign for the Mulhoney Community Center. Around the corner, a relic from the Golden Age of Cuteness—the Tick Tock Clock Shop. Noisy dairy trucks rumbled by us.

No subways. No sushi.

I sank in the front seat.

"Give it time," Addie directed.

"I'm giving it time."

"And I'm Queen Victoria."

You've Almost Reached the Best Diner in America.

Addie followed the arrow, muttering.

That's when I saw the two-story white frame building with the bright red double stairways descending from the glass door—one from the left, one from the right. An American flag waving from a flagpole. A walk of flowering trees circled toward the back. Every window had a flower box packed with blossoms. Above the front porch hung a big sign: Welcome Stairways.

Addie pointed to a balcony with big windows. "Our apartment's up there, I think."

It was 5:00 P.M. Addie parked the Buick with the U-Haul in the back of the Welcome Stairways. The lot was almost full—a good sign.

"It'll be full up and then some when I start cooking," Addie announced.

In the car waiting. It's what we always do before we start at a new place—sneak up on it—read the faces of the people coming out. It was the first time Addie hadn't visited a place she was going to work at. All she'd done was talk to the owner on the phone. Addie studied the two men coming through the back door, toothpicks in their mouths, not talking.

Not talking after a meal is serious. If people have really gotten something nourishing, it opens their personalities to the experience. The men got into a battered pickup silently and pulled away.

"Not too impressive," Addie said.

We watched as a woman and a teenage boy came out, talking a little, but not with animation.

"If they'd been fed properly it would show in their relationship." Addie opened the car door, marched toward the diner and said what all missionaries must say when they start in a new place.

"Lord in heaven, I've got my work cut out for me here."

3

We were sitting in a booth by the window, reading the list of daily specials.

"Meat, potatoes, and too much cheese," Addie muttered.

Three antique ceiling fans blew a gentle breeze through the diner: Everything seemed shiny and freshly painted white. There was a hooked rug of brilliant colors hanging on a wall, the booths by the windows had big blue seat cushions you just sank into. The counter sat twelve—good size, but manageable; behind the counter was a long shelf stocked with bottles of every kind of hot sauce known to man from Satan's Red-Hot Revenge to Texas Tabasco Terror. Black-and-white-checkerboard linoleum.

Definitely an above average diner.

"The dessert case is unacceptable," Addie snarled. "You going to put a pearl necklace from Tiffany's inside a plastic box?"

It was pretty puny. If you didn't know how Addie felt about her desserts, it would be hard to follow this.

"I've never been inside Tiffany's."

"I haven't either, but they know how to display their jewels, let me tell you."

A man with a sweet, broad face who didn't speak much English brought us water.

"Welcome, women," he said with a formal bow and then backed into a bus pan that was full of dirty dishes. A black waitress steadied it just before it would have crashed to the ground.

"Thank you, Lord," she said, laughing.

She was wearing a black skirt and a white blouse with the name *Flo* embroidered over her heart. Above her name she wore a little silver pin with the letters GOG inside a circle. She had a beautiful face and short, full hair. I liked her smile. She stood by our table—not there to rush us. I knew from Addie's notes that Flo was the floor manager.

"You nice folks decide?"

That made me grin. It takes Addie longer to warm up. It makes her nuts to be in a restaurant where she's not cooking.

Addie leaned forward in testing mode. "Now, when you say here 'pot roast with whipped potatoes,' are those potatoes whipped each day by hand or do you use the leftovers for a few days in a row?"

"We'll use the leftover whips in a shepherd's pie and in potato croquettes, but not on a dinner plate with pot roast. You know your way around a menu, don't you?"

Addie's blue eyes flickered in respect for Flo. "I'll have the pot roast, but I'd like the gravy on the side, and I'll have the mixed vegetables if they're fresh, but if not, I'll have the salad."

"What kind of dressing on the salad?" Flo asked, laughing.

Addie grinned back at Flo's command. "Russian."

"Yes?" The man with the sweet, broad face came instantly to our table.

Flo laughed gently and grabbed his hand. "Yuri here's from Russia. He thought you were calling him."

Flo walked him back to the kitchen. "Russian's not just a person, honey. It's a kind of salad dressing." Flo got salads from the case; poured dressing on them. "You're a Russian, and this is called Russian, too."

Yuri took a step backward, unsure.

She grinned. "It's a crazy world."

Yuri's eyebrows furrowed. "Crazy, yes."

Flo brought our salads, crisp and fresh, just as the door opened and eight big men came inside wearing VOTE FOR ELI MILLSTONE campaign buttons. One of the men handed a VOTE FOR ELI MILLSTONE poster to Flo and instructed her to put it in the window.

Flo said, "Langley, you know G.T. won't go for that. You'd better wait till he comes in tomorrow morning and you can talk to him yourself. Yuri, set a table, please, for these gentlemen."

"Welcome, men." Yuri pushed two tables together, brought place settings, got water and menus. The men sat down without thanking him.

"Coffee, men?"

"It true you from Russia?" one of the men asked Yuri.

"I leave Russia, yes."

"Well, that's kinda obvious," said another man, and the others laughed.

Yuri stood there laughing, too; he didn't know they were making fun of him. That made the others laugh harder.

Addie touched Yuri's arm. "Coffee, please," she asked sweetly. She didn't drink coffee at night; I knew she'd done it to get him away from that table.

Vote for Eli Millstone.

Whoever he was, already I didn't like him.

"Sweet Jesus." Addie flopped down on the stairs leading up to our apartment over the Welcome Stairways. We were trying to carry our small couch up the staircase. Being young and vital, I had more of the couch weight.

"Tell me the truth, Hope, what did you think of that meal we had tonight? I thought it was average."

"Let's just get the couch upstairs and—"

Addie picked up her end and huffed up the stairs. "I wonder if they can handle me introducing the butterscotch cream pie and the deep-dish apple in the same week."

"Could we do this a little quicker?"

"You can't overwhelm customers with too much at—"

"I'm going to drop the couch, Addie. It will fall on me and I'll die."

"Why didn't you say something before?" She eased the door open and pushed the couch through it to a very large room with white curtains.

I put down my end and fell to the floor to make a point.

Addie doesn't always pick up on subtle, except in seasonings.

*   *   *

We were set to meet with G. T. Stoop tomorrow morning.

Addie was sitting on the couch making notes on how to introduce her brand of revolutionary comfort food to the Welcome Stairways.

I'd written out my favorite definition of my name on a three-by-five card; I needed extra help in the hoping department.

From Webster's collegiate dictionary: *Hope—to cherish a desire with expectation of fulfillment.*

I hope, I hope, I hope this will all turn out for good.

I'd hoped for that very same thing at the Blue Box.

Some hopes just get pulverized.

I looked at myself in the big mirror we'd leaned against the wall, cocked my head, and smiled engagingly. My pearly white teeth are my best feature.

Next best is my curly brown hair that dusts my shoulders—except for my bangs that are too long and hide my eyebrows which were perfectly arched by God. I have a round face (a sweet face, people say) with no discernible cheekbones. My skin is pale, my eyes are light blue like my mother's. I'm five-eight, three inches taller than Addie, which gives me no power in our relationship. Miriam Lahey is two inches taller than her mother, which gives her a true advantage whenever they scream at each other.

I wrapped myself in a blanket so that only my eyes and nose were visible and wondered if the police would ever catch up with Gleason Beal, the King of Falsehood.

I should have been able to see the fakeness in him, even though Addie said that's not true.

"He was a con man, Hope. Pretended to be something that he wasn't."

I'll say.

He pretended to be my friend.

He told me one of the saddest things in his life was that he never had a daughter.

Addie shook out her graying brown ponytail. Folded her strong, muscled arms. She had strong arms like a wrestler from lugging all those kitchen pots around.

"Hope, I know Gleason Beal did a number on your head. That man took our money and our jobs, but let's not give him anything else. Not our minds, our hearts, or our souls. He's not worth it." She took her industrial-strength nightgown out of her suitcase. "We're not going to hide from the truth. This is probably the hardest move we've made together, honey, but we're going to give it all we've got to make it work, and if it still doesn't fit, we'll decide what to do. We won't stay someplace that isn't right forever. I promise."

I nodded from under my protective cloak.

Addie always keeps her promises.

That's why my mother gave me to her.

G. T. Stoop had a toothpick in his mouth and a mess of eggs on the grill. He had just folded over three cheddar omelets with bacon and had a strip steak sizzling next to a fat slab of ham. Addie and I were standing behind him in the big galley kitchen next to a huge pot of simmering onion soup that was making me hungry, even though I'd just stuffed myself beyond good sense with chocolate chip pancakes. A pale waitress with carrot-top hair called in "a short stack," which is restaurant-speak for a small order of pancakes. G. T. Stoop shook seasoned salt on the steak, put it on a plate with eggs, beans, and a side of cornbread, dinged a bell, put the order up by the galley window, and shouted, "Come get this miracle breakfast, Florence, before I eat it myself!"

Flo, our waitress from last night, shouted across the room. "G.T., back off from that man's plate and behave yourself."

He grinned, wiggled his toothpick. "I'm not so good at that." He had a big, deep voice.

"Lord, don't I know it." Flo was at the galley window now,

getting her order. She put the plate in front of a big man sitting at the counter.

G. T. Stoop threw his spatula up in the air and caught it. "Eat that, Carl, and go do something significant with your day."

Carl raised his fork and knife happily, already chewing.

Everyone was laughing and eating.

I sure didn't feel like I was in the presence of a person who had cancer.

It was 6:30 A.M., the best time to see a diner because, as Addie always said, if the place isn't humming by then, the word hasn't gotten out yet.

Welcome Stairways was humming.

G. T. Stoop poured pancake batter on the griddle. He was medium height, bean thin with a square, gentle face, and totally bald. He had deep blue eyes that shone behind the wire rims perched on the end of his nose. He was wearing jeans, work boots, and a blue shirt with the cuffs rolled above his elbows—no apron. Addie always wore an apron. He was moving with the rhythm of the short-order dance—popped four pieces of bread in a toaster, slipped onions onto the side of the grill, poured batter into a waffle iron.

"I love the morning best," he said, smiling. "I already miss sweating back here six days a week, but you're going to elevate the food in this place like I never could, Addie, I know it."

Addie said, "I can add a frittata to your menu—eggs, potatoes, onions, and fresh herbs—give folks a nice change each day with different seasonings."

"That sounds good. But in this town let's call it an egg casserole."

Addie laughed. "I'll cook it. You name it."

He laughed back, flipped pancakes. "Now that's a partnership. Hope, how are you handling all this change coming up here?"

"I'm pretty adaptable." I always say that.

"To adapt is to overcome. That's what my barber used to say when I still had hair for him to cut." He spread butter on toast, sliced it fast, arranged it on plates with eggs and sausage; a slice of orange. "I remember my family moving in the middle of my junior year in high school. I wanted to kill my old man for doing that to me."

I put my hand on Addie's shoulder. "I decided to let her live."

Brilliant, Hope. The man has cancer.

I winced. "I didn't mean that the wrong way." Addie gave me one of her furrowed-brow looks, but G. T. Stoop waved his spatula.

"Be yourself around me. I don't give many orders, but that's one of them." He flipped a sausage to me backhanded. I caught it in midair, which was very cool. "Don't have to mince your words either," he added. "The only thing we mince around here is garlic."

I smiled, ate the sausage. Sweet and mapley.

"I'm not dead yet," he said, placing three plates at the galley window. "Am I, Florence?"

Flo grabbed the plates, smiled big at us, and said, "G.T., you're going to outlive us all."

"That's my plan." He layered Canadian bacon on the grill, pressed it down with his spatula. His eyes crackled when he smiled.

I bit my lip even though Addie winked at me. This kind of talk was going to take some getting used to.

A very tall guy—six-four at least—came into the kitchen carrying a bowl of chopped green and red peppers. He looked a little older than me and was the most angular person I'd ever seen—every bit of him seemed to have pointy edges. He had wavy black hair and amazingly thick eyebrows. He was wearing jeans, a black T-shirt, and sneakers. I'd place him, at first glance, around a 6.7 on Jocelyn Lindstrom's male cuteness scale. Ten being a rugged yet sensitive world-class surfer (preferably wet); one being a toad. He nodded to me and Addie. "I'm Braverman."

"Grill man supreme," added G.T. "Second in command in this kitchen, with nerves of steel."

Braverman took down a plate of home fries on a shelf by the grill and raised one eyebrow, half smiling.

"These women are going to set us straight." G.T. placed cinnamon apples in four pancakes, flipped them perfectly, and ran his hand across his bare head. "You know, there's benefits to everything. Now that I lost my hair to the chemotherapy, I don't worry about it getting in the food."

I smiled nervously.

Flo came into the kitchen laughing and said we'd set her up good last night and she appreciated the big tip. We met Lou Ellen, the waitress with the carrot-top hair. She looked me up and down, not impressed.

"You waitressed before?"

I looked her smack in the eye. "I've got eighteen months

experience waitressing in the best diner in Brooklyn, New York, and before that—"

"Counter or tables?" Lou Ellen interrupted. She had a pinched-together face.

"Both."

"How busy did it get?"

"They'd be standing out in a line on the weekends and I couldn't go to the bathroom for five hours straight even if I had to, it was so jammed."

"I've been waitressing ten years," she snapped back.

I didn't ask how long she could hold it.

She layered three pancake platters on her left arm (I can carry five) and headed off to a booth in the corner. Addie was examining a piece of blueberry coffee cake on a plate the way a scientist studies a petri dish.

"We bake it ourselves here every morning," G. T. Stoop said proudly. "It sells pretty good."

"Really . . ." Addie took her fork and cut through the center of the cake, flicked off some crumbs. I knew what she was thinking.

Dry.

She took a bite, chewed it slowly, no expression on her face. Addie tastes food the way some people play poker.

"It's my mother's recipe," he added.

"And I'm sure she is a fine, upstanding woman," Addie said. "But her coffee cake is dry."

He looked up to the ceiling, laughed deep. "Lord, what have I done bringing this woman up here?"

"I'm here," Addie replied, "so you can rest easy."

"I don't expect that's going to happen." He handed her a big chain of keys. "You keep this place running smooth and I'll attend to other matters."

Addie jingled them. "It'll be like a knife going through maple butter."

Braverman stood to the side studying the orders G.T. was cooking. G.T. raised his spatula, Braverman nodded, eyes on the grill. And like air traffic controllers changing shifts, G.T. moved from the grill, Braverman took his place, and he started flipping pancakes, turning bacon, frying eggs. Not one yolk was broken in the process.

Flo was listening behind the counter. "G.T., you've been cooking up something for over a month. What is it?"

"You'll find out tomorrow, Florence. After the parade."

As parades go, it's pretty hard to impress a New Yorker. For my money, unless you've got huge Garfield and Big Bird balloons flapping in the wind ten floors up, you don't call yourself a parade. You're a gathering.

I wasn't much in the mood for a gathering.

I'd been dragged here.

Addie and I were standing on the corner of Pine and Magellan Streets by Scarlotti's World of Cheese, which was offering a fifteen percent discount to all veterans for the three-day weekend. People were lined four deep in the street. I was studying the Welcome Stairways menu so I wouldn't look like an amateur when I started work the next morning. Nothing can slow you up faster than not knowing the menu.

"That's Deena's blood in you," Addie remarked. "She always knew the menu like the back of her hand."

Mom is an overachieving waitress like me. In her last Christmas letter she wrote that she'd been thinking about the decisions she'd made in life and felt that the best one had been to stay in waitressing: "No matter what happens in the world, from war breaking out to computers taking over our minds and bodies, there's always going to be a need for a good waitress who can keep the coffee coming and add up the check in her head."

A mediocre band stumbled by—the Mulhoney High School Marauders—my new school. Purple-and-gold uniforms. I scanned their faces to find kindred spirits. It's hard to tell people's true nature when they're playing Sousa.

Next, Vietnam vets in combat fatigues; World War II veterans rode behind them, waving flags. I applauded as they went by. Antique cars/scout troops/clowns/a happy float with happy farmers with a banner for the REAL FRESH DAIRY.

Another float—red, white, and blue—flags flapping, streamers streaming. A man in a red jacket and khakis waving to the crowd. Above him a bold banner: ELECT ELI MILLSTONE FOR MAYOR IF YOU CARE ABOUT MULHONEY. Some of the men I'd seen in the diner last night walked beside the float like bodyguards.

A flurry of movement beside me. Braverman. He watched the Millstone float with angry eyes.

"He's been mayor for eight years," Braverman said.

"Who's running against him?"

"Nobody. He's too powerful."

A plump, red-faced man in a law enforcement uniform shouted, "Move it back, people. Move it back on the curb." The name above his badge read *Sheriff L. Greebs.*

A harsh-looking man in a MILLSTONE T-shirt was working the crowd, clapping his hands over his head. "Let's hear it for four more years for Mayor Eli Millstone, the only choice for Mulhoney!"

Just about everyone was clapping except me, Addie, and Braverman.

"You're not clapping for the mayor," the man said to Braverman.

"That's right," Braverman shot back. The muscles in his neck stuck out when he said it. The man stared at him and eventually moved off. Then that man looked back and stared at me, too.

A shiver of fear went through me.

Miss Pittypat's Tap Dancing Darlings were arriving on the stage that was set up in the park off Grimes Square. There were about twelve children in black-and-yellow bumblebee costumes with bouncing antennae. They formed a questionable line and began their big number, which required intense concentration because in addition to tap tap tapping, they also had to sing:

> *Hello, how are ya?*
> *We're really glad to see ya.*
> *We really want to tell ya, hello!*

I longed for Manhattan and the jazz fusion street band that played in Times Square.

Addie and I stood by a white gazebo as the Dancing Darlings scurried off to frenzied applause. Mayor Millstone was master of ceremonies. His round stomach didn't move an inch when he laughed. To quote Shirley Polanski, head waitress at the Humdinger Diner: "Beware of a big man whose stomach doesn't move when he laughs."

I think a Chinese philosopher said it first, but these things trickle down to the food service community.

G. T. Stoop walked to the stage. "Eli, I'd like to make an announcement."

The mayor looked surprised. "Well, sure thing, G.T. What about?"

"I'll just say it once, if that's okay."

G.T. stood at the microphone not talking for the longest time. The sun beat down on his shiny head. I wondered what it was like to lose your hair.

"Afternoon, folks."

People shushed their children.

"Most of you know what's going on with me, and some of you don't. I wouldn't be making a public announcement about it except for you needing to know what I'm planning to do. When I was diagnosed with leukemia earlier this year, I realized I couldn't stand at the short-order grill for ten hours a day anymore. I needed to get myself more of a desk job." He chuckled. "So I've decided to run for mayor."

A deep shock fell on the crowd. Eli Millstone's smile evaporated. I looked at Addie, who'd turned stone still.

"Now I didn't put together one of those exploratory committees to tell me if I should do this. The way I see it, you're either open for business or you're not. But those of you who've stared down a thing like cancer know what happens when you get this kind of news about your health. At first, you can't believe it; after that, the fear gets pretty strong. I'm fifty-four years old. I never once felt the need to rush through life until now."

Eli Millstone's eyes narrowed.

"I've learned things with this disease I never would have otherwise. Mostly I've learned how important it is to do the right thing, no matter who opposes you."

He rubbed his hand over his bald head. "I'm in this race to try to bring unity and fairness to our town. For my money, we have too many warring factions here—people who don't want the Real Fresh Dairy to expand any further; people who do. People who want better day care for our families; people who don't. People who think the schools are just fine the way they are; people who are worried about the overcrowding. And what's happened is we've pulled off into our separate corners and nothing's getting done. We need to renovate that broken-down community center of ours and use it to draw people together again. We need to develop better day care facilities for the families in this area because children are our future. We need to use more of our money to help the poor of Mulhoney get a leg up. We need to make sure our young people get jobs so that every single one of them who wants to can earn money for college."

"G.T.!" Eli Millstone was at his shoulder, face flushed. "Those are sweet dreams and I share every one. Just how *high* are you suggesting we raise these good people's taxes to get the money to pay for all this?"

A ripple of worry hit the crowd.

G.T. looked at the mayor. "Eli, since you brought it up, here's my plan. The biggest company in town, the Real Fresh Dairy, hasn't paid any local taxes for five years and owes three-quarters of a million dollars in back tax revenue. I'd say collecting that money is a good place to start."

People looked at each other and gasped.

Millstone sputtered, "I don't know where you're getting your information, G.T., but it's as bogus as a barking cat!"

"I just went to the tax assessor's office, Eli. I had to search through some big computer printouts, but the facts are there for anyone to see."

"You're lying!"

"No sir." G.T. set his jaw. "Our roads are cracking because dairy trucks are carrying loads heavier than our streets can handle. We have residents in the south end who can't sleep at night because those trucks are rumbling by their windows, taking illegal shortcuts to the interstate to save gas and time. I say we levy a fat fine against that business until they obey the law. We can use that money to fix the roads and help our people."

Braverman let out a whoop and started clapping. Others joined him.

Millstone's face had splotches of purple rage. He grabbed the mike.

"We are assessing the traffic-flow situation in this town,

G.T. Town business is a little more complicated than flipping burgers on a grill, which is what you've been doing for as long as I can remember."

"Oh," G.T. said, laughing, "you learn courage and decision making quick when you've got two dozen burgers on the grill."

People laughed good at that one.

Braverman put two fingers in his mouth and whistled loud. I wish I could whistle like that.

Eli Millstone was working hard to overcome his irritation. His smile got bigger, his face muscles got stiffer, he grabbed the microphone and laughed deep.

"How 'bout we stop wasting everyone's time with nonsense and start talking *real* issues? I'm running on my record. The Real Fresh Dairy has put this town on the map, folks, and I brought them here. Look around and see the progress. Is Mulhoney a bigger, more bustling place than it was eight years ago? Have living conditions improved? Are there more jobs? Is there more business for our local stores? You bet your boots, and it will continue into my third term and beyond. I'm mighty proud of my accomplishments."

The men who were walking by Eli Millstone's float started applauding loudly.

G.T. raised his voice: "Let's not forget Mulhoney's family-run dairies that went out of business when the Real Fresh Dairy came to town."

Millstone waved that off. "If they'd been better-managed businesses, they would have survived."

"Raising their property taxes sky high was what killed

them." G.T. looked straight at him. "Then the Real Fresh Dairy swooped down and bought their land cheap."

"You're living in La-La Land, *mister*." The Mayor motioned stiffly to Miss Pittypat, who shoved the Dancing Darlings onstage for an insect extravaganza number featuring "Eensy Weensy Spider" and "Glow Worm."

Addie turned to me. "G. T. Stoop's crazy as a loon! He's going to be dead in a month with all this stress!"

I gulped.

G.T. walked off the stage and headed toward us. "I think that went pretty well," he said, looking at Addie, who didn't speak. "I'm sure glad you're here to run things, Addie, so I can go make a fool of myself in politics."

Addie gave a slight nod. I wasn't sure if she was acknowledging her ability to run things or him being a fool.

And G. T. Stoop strode smiling through the crowd that parted for him like the Red Sea did for Moses.

5

Back at the Welcome Stairways we were deep in the weeds—that's diner language for way too busy. Memorial Day always brings the hungry hordes, but after G.T.'s announcement people were pushing into the place like we were giving away free food. Addie was trying to handle herself in an unfamiliar kitchen. People were shouting questions at G.T., who was standing under one of the big antique ceiling fans trying to answer. Lou Ellen tripped over a man's leg and let a nacho plate with meat, beans, and guacamole go sailing. It looked like the best any of us could hope for was survival.

Flo throws me a white apron.

Lou Ellen plunks an order pad in my hand. "We'll see what you're made of. Take the counter."

Even when you're not in school, life is a test.

Twelve hungry people at the counter. First, my effervescent smile.

I am your friend, not your foe.

Second, go for pity.

"This is my first day and I don't know where anything is, but I promise you I'll find it. How many would like coffee?"

Seven hands go up and I get coffee, racing past Lou Ellen, who is staring at me. I carry six coffee cups with saucers in my left hand, piled on two by two, without spilling a drop; take the seventh cup in my right hand and deliver the goods.

People are shouting orders at me so fast I can't think. I run to the galley window to call them in.

Addie's snarling in the kitchen, opening refrigerator doors, saying she can't sauté a chicken breast if she can't find one, now can she? Braverman's watching the grill, flipping burgers, calmly telling her where things are.

"Ordering pork-chop specials on three," I say. Braverman nods, raises a thick eyebrow.

Addie slams a pan.

I deliver a taco salad and a burger to the table near the front door like it gives me sheer delight to do it.

Sheriff L. Greebs storms into the diner. "You're over the safety limit for the number of persons that can be in this establishment." He motions to the line waiting near the register. "Move it outside, people, or I'll have to shut this place down."

He leads the disgruntled out the door.

A man shouts from across the room. "G.T., how are you going to handle the stress of campaigning and being mayor if you're fighting for your life?"

G.T. leans against the dessert case across from the register. "Because I'm more interested in living than in dying. And I want to bring as much healthy change into this town as I can before I go. I'm a short-order cook, Morgan. I always do more than one thing at a time."

Everyone starts laughing.

I'm pouring coffee. The secret when you're in the weeds is to keep the coffee coming.

Flo is racing from the kitchen with her arm full of burger specials and not dropping one french fry. I'm taking orders, getting food, squeezing past people, experiencing the fierceness of food service. I look out the window. The line to get in the diner is curling around the block.

Yuri rolls his eyes. "Lines like Russia." He rushes to a booth with water and setups.

"Take booth eight," Lou Ellen snaps at me like I was born knowing where it is. She points to the six-top by the register. A six-top is a table that seats six people.

I'm there. Mercifully, they order fast.

I pour more coffee for the people in the corner booth in Lou Ellen's station. She stalks me into the kitchen.

"That's my table."

"I was trying to help."

"I take care of my tables."

Then why were they out of coffee?

A woman perched at the counter wearing a straw hat and a big flowered dress shouts, "Aren't there laws in this country that say people running for elected office have to be healthy?"

G.T. smiles. "Cecelia, our town charter says anyone can run for mayor who's a resident, thirty years of age and up, and a U.S. citizen."

She writes that down on her notepad and nods at me. "Cecelia Culpepper. Editor of the *Mulhoney Messenger*."

"Hope Yancey."

"Nice name, kid."

I'm running everywhere juggling thirty-five things in my head, fully focused, heart pounding. I wish I knew the menu better, but you've got to start somewhere and it might as well be hard and fast.

A kid throws his spoon at his baby sister. I'm there to catch it before disaster. I hand it to his mother, who looks at me gratefully.

Full-service waitressing. We feed, protect, and defend.

Flo rushes past me, laughing. "You're getting into it."

I grin. "Oh yeah."

Braverman shouts, "Burger specials on four up and ready." That's me. I rush to the galley window, layer the plates on my left arm. A woman says, "G.T., you have no political experience. Why should we vote for you?"

G.T. says he'd been on the school board, he helped get the emergency health center built. He's lived in this town for twenty-five years.

"How long have you known about the dairy's unpaid taxes?" a man shouts.

"Just before Christmas last year," G.T. explains. "I tried to see Eli about it three times, but he wouldn't meet with me. I decided the only thing left to do was make a public statement. But leukemia hit. It was all I could focus on for a time. I apologize to all of you for being selfish."

Everyone starts talking at once.

A hand on my shoulder. It's Flo. She's introducing me to her friend Brenda Babcock, sheriff's deputy. Deputy Babcock is close to the most beautiful African-American woman I've ever seen—her cheekbones were to die for.

"Brenda just got transferred here last month from Minneapolis. She's the toughest law enforcement officer on God's earth."

"I crush bad guys under my heel." Brenda Babcock grins and shakes my hand. "Seems we've come to town at an interesting time, Hope."

I smile back at her. "I guess so."

I look at the line outside waiting to get into the diner. Sheriff L. Greebs is glaring at people like a prison guard.

"G.T.," an old woman shouts. "How sick are you?"

"I've had one round of chemotherapy, Emma. I'm hoping it will put me into remission."

"What if it doesn't?" someone yells.

"Then I'll do it again."

Man.

I push my bangs back. Face the counter. A big guy with a long face slides onto a stool—doesn't look left or right—grabs the menu. He's there to eat and get out. I go up to him, smile glowing.

"How are things with you, sir?"

"Fine." He says it flat. "Coffee black. BLT."

Now my heart tells me this guy needs more in life, so I take a shot. "You ever had a cheddar burger with grilled onions and mushrooms on pumpernickel, sir?"

That takes a minute to sink in.

Then he slaps the counter, grinning. "Bring it on."

I sense he needs more.

"You want a malt with that, by any chance?"

He did, of course. *"Chocolate,"* he says, beaming like a kid.

Now he's loosening up.

It's a privilege to touch humanity in such a fashion.

I race to the kitchen window, call the order in.

G.T. is holding up a wad of paper. "My petition's right here if anyone wants to sign it. The Election Board says I need two hundred registered voters to get on the ballot officially."

Not many people come forward.

An old man with a wrinkled face scans the petition. "I don't know, G.T. I get a lot of business at my store from the dairy. I think signing this might hurt me."

"It might at that," G.T. acknowledges.

"I've got to think about it, too," says a woman. "My husband and son work at the dairy . . ."

Sheriff Greebs is in the doorway.

The woman sees him. "And they love their jobs," she says nervously. "They really do!"

"I'll sign that thing." The black man I'd seen driving the church van when we first came into town strides forward, bringing bolts of energy with him. He has a fat mustache peppered with gray.

Flo is standing behind me. "That's Pastor Al B. Hall of my church. They're real good friends."

"I sure appreciate it, Al," G.T. says.

Pastor Hall takes the petition. He pushes back his hat and looks at G.T. "You got any more surprises for today?"

"Maybe." G.T. grins.

Pastor Hall signs the petition, slaps it in G.T.'s hands, takes him by the elbow, and yanks him toward the counter where I'm pouring coffee.

"You could have mentioned this to me," Pastor Hall whispers. "Good Lord, man."

"I figured you'd try to talk me out of it."

"You've got that right. You're always going off like a fool, not telling people what you're doing!"

"You going to vote for me, Al?"

"I'm going to *pray* for you."

"Afternoon, Pastor," says Flo sweetly, indicating with her eyes that the whole diner is trying to listen in.

The two men face the crowd, thump each other on the back, and smile.

And now several people with GOG T-shirts come up to sign; that brings a few more people. Flo stands in line.

I wish I was old enough to sign that petition. When you can carry five full dinner platters on your left arm, you should be able to vote, even if you're not eighteen.

It had been an exhausting Memorial Day. I'd gone through two order books and gotten all the food hot to the customers, except for the broiled chicken breast Mexicana that I had to send back to Braverman because he'd put cheddar cheese on the top even though I said hold the cheese. Being a grill man, he wasn't about to admit he was wrong. You can't argue in these instances—it wastes time. Speed and delivery are what makes a good waitress, and you learn to compromise along the way to get that food delivered and your customers taken care of. When I apologized to Braverman for the mistake, he nearly fell over. My mother taught me to do that on my thirteenth birthday—the last time I saw her. She said there are three hard and fast rules that every professional waitress has to follow:

(1) The customer is always right.

(2) The cook is always right.

(3) If the customer and the cook disagree, and you can't settle it, your tip is history.

I have those rules in my Best of Mom book that Addie made me keep from the time I was little. Addie said even though my mother hardly came around, she was still an important part of my life, and it was up to me to save and remember the things she passed on.

On cheap tippers: "Don't take it personally; they were deprived somehow as children."

On low-fat entrees: "They sell well enough, but nobody's too happy after the meal."

On regular customers: "Talk to them, remember what they say, and ask them about it tomorrow."

On men: "They tip better when they're not with their girlfriends."

On children in restaurants: "Play up to them. Their parents love it."

I've kept all the Christmas letters she sends, too. I guess I appreciate the contact, but it's weird having a pen parent. I didn't get the Christmas letter once and got worried. It came on Groundhog Day. Mom had met the man of her dreams in Las Vegas, a blackjack dealer named Roberto. She was in such bliss she got nothing done until she realized what a slimeball he was and told him to take a hike. She wrote "Fa la la la la la la la la" at the bottom, which is how Mom sees a lot of life.

The last time I saw her she looked so uncomfortable I thought she was going to jump out the window.

She told me I looked good, but didn't make eye contact.

She told me it's okay I changed my name and kept calling me Tulip.

She told me she loved me and never came back.

Staring down hard truth takes guts. Once Addie told me that unless a genuine miracle happened, it was a safe bet that Mom wasn't going to change.

"I know it's hard to handle," Addie started, "but if I lie to you now it's only going to make things worse later on. It doesn't mean Deena doesn't love you. It means she doesn't have the tools she needs to be the kind of mother you want her to be. She didn't lose them somewhere along the way, honey. She never had them to begin with."

The well was dry—that's what I concluded. I wrote a poem about it once—free verse—I can't rhyme for anything.

> *I had expected the well to be full for some reason.*
> *Not that it had ever been before.*
> *I kept looking for signs of water in the dark insides.*
> *I heard my bucket clank as it hit*
> *Against the walls that held nothing.*
> *I looked at the bucket that came up empty*
> *And made a decision that changed my life.*
> *I will keep my bucket and find another well.*

Harrison said I should submit it to the poetry journal at school, but I never did. He said I should give it to my English teacher for extra credit, but this wasn't something I wanted published or graded. Harrison wrote a two-page poem about his deep feelings of loss when his dog Filbert died, and Mrs. Minerva, the creative writing teacher, gave it a B-minus. Do you know what that does to a person to get a B-minus in Grief?

I was filling saltshakers and napkin holders, wondering if G. T. Stoop was going to kill himself with this campaign. Wondering if there were any interesting teenagers in such a dinky dairy town.

Braverman walked out from the kitchen holding a stack of papers with lines on them. "We need to help G.T. get this petition signed. There's a bunch of us going out tomorrow to start."

A creaking door of friendship was opening. I knew zip about politics, but admitting that would not have been shrewd. "I want to help. Is it okay I can't vote yet?"

He looked at me like cooks do when the server before them has done something stupid.

I guess that meant it was okay.

"What if someone asks me a question?"

Braverman leaned against the counter. "Tell them G. T. Stoop has the courage to face anything in this world and come out ahead, and *that's* what this town needs."

I could tell by his face that he meant what he said. "I guess you know him pretty well."

"When my mom was out of work, G.T. gave me a job waiting tables, then he taught me to cook."

"Wow."

Braverman was zeroing in on a ketchup bottle.

A long, weird silence.

"So, Braverman. Do you ... ah ... go to the high school?"

"I graduated last year."

"You go to college around here?"

"I can't go to college right now."

Dumb, Hope.

He shuffled the petitions. "You know how to lock up?"

"I've got the key. Flo showed me."

"The back door sticks."

"Okay."

He walked out the door before I could apologize.

My life, so far, in Wisconsin:

Worked all day.

Irritated the cook.

"Good night, Braverman," I said to the closed front door.

I walked in the back to lock up, put the key in the lock, jiggled it like Flo showed me. Jiggled it again. Again.

It wouldn't lock.

I tried for ten minutes every which way.

I felt like I used to when I was little and we'd just moved. I'd be standing in some new hall holding my new apartment key and not be able to open my new front door.

"Come on!" I jiggled the stupid thing.

I hit the door hard like I used to, felt the sting in my hand.

I felt like crying. I didn't want to be here.

A light went on behind me.

I stiffened.

"I have trouble with that back door, too." It was G.T. He walked right up to me, took the key. "I am one sorry mess with keys. On my wedding day I locked my keys in my truck along with my rented tuxedo. Had to kick in the window of that pickup just to get married." He hit the door, jiggled the key a few times. Finally the lock clicked shut. He looked at me, smiling. "Best not mention that on the campaign trail. Cancer and key dysfunction might be more than the voters can handle."

I laughed.

"Go on upstairs and get some sleep now."

"Thanks." I headed for the door.

"You're a fine waitress, Hope. You know how to connect with the people."

I looked back at him, grinning.

There wasn't a better thing that a boss could have said.

6

Grimes Square, o-eight-hundred.

I was with a group consisting of Braverman and four teenagers from Mulhoney High, members of the Students for Political Freedom Coalition. Adam Pulver, pug-faced president of the club, shook my hand like he was running for Congress—a force.

Adam handed out clipboards with petitions and pens and made sure everyone knew the rules.

Only registered voters from town can sign.

Only legible signatures are accepted.

Always thank people for their time whether they've signed or not, even if they are jerks and morons.

Braverman tossed a peanut in the air and caught it in his mouth.

Adam raised his mechanical pencil. "If *any* information is wrong on these petitions, if a person signs who thinks he's registered and isn't, if an address is wrong, whatever, the signature doesn't count. Too many of those and we could get kicked off the ballot. I've seen it happen again and again."

Again and again was doubtful since Adam was, maybe, seventeen.

More teenagers were showing up to get petitions. It didn't take long to find out why.

Leon: "G.T. gave me a job busing tables when my dad had an accident and couldn't work."

Jillian: "G.T. let my cousins live in his extra apartment when they couldn't pay the rent on their house."

Brice: "G.T. sent food every week to my family when my mom was in the hospital."

Adam Pulver faced the group. "It's not going to be easy out there today. But remember, our cause is just." He squinted into the sun like a hard-bitten campaign pro and said with a slight crack in his voice, "Now let's get out there and do something for America."

"He always says that," Jillian whispered to me.

Doing something for America is trickier than it sounds.

"You tell me what this world's coming to," a plump woman with a plump child said to me, "when the voters' choice for mayor is between a dying man and a crook."

"Well . . ." I began.

"I've known G.T. for twenty-five years," the plump woman continued, "and there's no denying he's a fine man, but that doesn't qualify him to be running for mayor with no experience and leukemia to boot."

She had a point there.

I looked desperately around. Braverman was behind me listening in.

Help, I mouthed.

"G.T.'s been on the school board," Braverman countered. "He helped us get those dangerous steps repaired at the high school. He brings food to people when they're having financial trouble."

"That's true."

"He worked hard to get that emergency medical center in town so people don't have to drive twenty-five miles to the nearest hospital."

Braverman held out the petition, said her signature just allowed G.T. to be on the ballot officially.

The woman's child drooled on the petition. She signed.

"Thank you!" Braverman wiped the paper on his leg. "You won't be sorry."

"I'm sorry every day of my life, young man." She plodded off.

Encouraged by Braverman's victory, I approached a man walking toward me. He was holding the hand of a little boy who looked just like him.

I flashed my toothpaste-ad smile. "Excuse me, sir, but we're out collecting signatures from registered voters to get G. T. Stoop on the ballot for mayor and I was wondering if you—"

The man kept walking.

"—might want to sign this so that G.T. can—"

The man walked faster; the boy was running to keep up. "You want me to vote for some guy who flips burgers on a grill and who's half dead with leukemia? You want to sell me some desert real estate in the rain forest while you're at it?"

Excuse me for breathing, but I don't think a father should be acting like that in front of his son!

I watched that man turn the corner fast.

I'll bet you hard cash that my father would never do anything like that.

Braverman was standing in front of me, casting a shadow. "Come on. We can team up."

The rest of the morning went down like cold rolls with a hot meal.

We knocked on doors and got seven slammed in our face.

A mother holding a shrieking infant asked if we baby-sat.

An old man holding a rifle told us to get off his property. We obeyed instantly.

Three women said G.T. was a fine man, but their husbands needed their jobs at the dairy.

It's amazing how many ways people can tell you to buzz off.

We'd had enough for one day.

The humidity made everything seem heavy. The hot sun beat down. Braverman and I were walking through Grimes Square. I was hungry. In New York you could always get a hot dog from a street vendor. No street meat here. A store called Wisconsin Giftique had a window display with small colored cheeses in the shape of farm animals. I felt like Dorothy plopped down in Munchkin Land.

A noisy dairy truck rumbled by too fast. Painted on the side: MILK DOESN'T GET ANY FRESHER THAN THIS. JUST ASK THE COW. I turned to Braverman. "What's with the big, bad dairy?"

Braverman threw a stick. "That's our mystery around here. Some people say they funded Millstone's campaign and he lets them do whatever they want. I've heard they basically own the people who work for them. Brice's dad was a factory manager there for a while. His boss told him he had to contribute to Millstone's campaign."

"What did he do?"

"He quit."

Braverman stopped at a long driveway that led to a huge new house with white pillars. "That's the mayor's new place."

"Wow." I looked at the three-car attached garage, the baby evergreens lining the walk.

"He built it last year. He said his wife inherited a ton of money." Braverman put his hand over his heart. "How else could a small-town mayor afford a place like this?"

"What do you mean?"

Braverman's jaw locked. "Maybe Millstone's lying."

"You think the dairy gave him the money?"

"I think there's a reason the Real Fresh Dairy does whatever it wants to around here. Cranston Broom's the owner, and he knows how to play it. He and Millstone are big buddies—they play golf, go deep-sea fishing. Broom's dairy workers clean up the park by the railroad tracks, his trucks deliver free milk to the schools. So people let them alone."

I thought of little kids drinking tainted milk. I thought of Gleason Beal hiring me at fifteen and giving me all that responsibility opening up on the weekends. I thought of the raise he gave me right before he stole our money, which, of course, was his way of taking the raise back.

It was probably easier in the old days when the bad guys rode into town wearing black capes or whatever bad guys wore and the milk cows were owned by honest people. Right off the bat, you'd know who you were dealing with.

Now everybody dresses alike. That's the problem with progress.

The yo-yo was doing amazing things.

A perfect double loop Round the World.

The longest Walk the Dog I'd ever witnessed.

Braverman flicked his wrist and the orange Duncan snapped back in his hand.

"That was great, Braverman."

"I'm a little rusty."

That was rusty?

The muscles in his face looked chiseled out of rock. I think I had misjudged him on the male cuteness scale. I would definitely put him at a 7.4.

We were across the street from the Welcome Stairways. G.T. was sitting on a park bench in front of the diner talking to a few old people.

I had to ask. "Do you know how G.T.'s doing, Braverman?"

Yo-yo in the pocket. Big sigh. "He's had a pretty rough time. The chemotherapy made him so tired. He couldn't be around people during part of it, which drove him crazy. He'd be stuck upstairs calling the diner to see if we were handling things." Braverman laughed. "I'd have the phone under my chin, trying to cook, telling him everything was under control when it wasn't."

"You really helped him."

He shrugged. "I just did my job. He's waiting to find out if he goes into remission."

"Remission means the cancer's gone, right?"

"Or gets better for a while. We'll take what we can get."

We walked closer.

"You want to know why to vote for a man who's fighting for his life?" we heard G.T. say. "Because no one understands how sweet life can be, how blessed every minute is, how important it is to say and do what's right while you've got the time, more than a person who's living with a short wick."

An old woman was hanging on his every word. I took a chance, handed her the petition.

"Are you a registered voter, ma'am?"

"I've been voting since Harry Truman took office."

She signed it, handed it to the woman next to her, who'd been voting, probably, since Abe Lincoln took office. Then three other people signed.

"Thank you, friends." G.T. got up, gave a weary smile, and walked slowly across the street and up the welcome stairways, head shining.

People are sneaky. A check of voter signatures proved this out.

Somebody signed, "Eleanor Roosevelt."

Somebody wrote, "When hell freezes over."

Some signatures were impossible to read.

I was sitting in the back booth with Braverman and Adam,

checking the petition names against the list of registered voters from the Board of Elections. Adam had gotten the most names today. He'd gone to the emergency medical center that G.T. helped get built and asked wounded people for their support. His petition had bloodstains on it. He said blood added to the glory of the fight.

Jillian and Brice ran into the diner. "We got twelve names at the A and P, but that creepy guy kept following us down the street." Brice pointed nervously out the window as a black funeral hearse parked in front of the Welcome Stairways like the darkest omen of what was to come.

The driver looked like an evil henchman. He was one of the men wearing a VOTE FOR ELI MILLSTONE button I'd seen in the diner the first night we'd gotten here.

Lou Ellen was taking her break, reading her personal copy of *Soap Opera Digest* like she'd be tested on every word. "Yuck," she said, looking out the window at the hearse. "Those things give me the creeps." Her face pinched together when she said it.

So far there was nothing about her I could find to like.

Braverman stormed to the window.

Adam marched behind him. "I could get a convict suit. Follow Millstone around. See how *he* likes it."

"The two of you sit down."

It was G.T.

"You know what bullies want. They want a rise out of you. That's what feeds them." G.T. took singles out of the cash register and started counting.

Braverman clenched his fists.

G.T. looked at us with such kindness in his face. "I'll tell you what my mother told me long ago. She was a good Quaker woman; listened for God to speak to her every day. She said you've got to love yourself with all your shortcomings, and you've got to love the world, no matter how bad it gets."

Boy, would I make a lousy Quaker.

Adam Pulver glared at the floor tile. "We're not going to win this way, G.T."

"Then the thing's not worth winning." G.T. put the money in the cash register and looked out the window as the hearse rounded the corner coming back for more.

7

It was night.

I had everything unpacked finally. Empty moving boxes piled in a heap—the cardboard symbols of starting over. (Harrison Beckworth-McCoy's line, not mine.)

My room: light yellow walls, blue rug, bed at an angle between the two windows; tangerine quilt with yellow piping.

Everything seemed like it belonged there.

Except me.

When does the magic hit in a new place and you suddenly fit in?

In Brooklyn it hit when I met Miriam. In Pensacola it hit when I got to be a waitress. In Atlanta it happened when I stopped fighting.

I studied the black leather boxing gloves hanging behind my bedroom door.

Not every girl can say that boxing saved her.

I learned to box when I was eleven. I thought it was just to do something physical, but Addie knew different. She had a policeman friend, Mickey Kazdan, who boxed. He'd take me to the ring and show me the moves—how to dance lightly around an opponent, how to protect my face, how to do quick jabs. I never fought anyone; I just punched the bag, swinging away until I was exhausted.

One day I went to the gym and was punching the big bag when a chord deep down in me connected to fury. I hit the bag harder, harder, tears streaming down my face. I was punching with jabs and rights and left hooks. I'm told I was saying, "You shouldn't have done it! You shouldn't have!" Mickey Kazdan stood by me telling people to back off.

"Punch it out, slugger, until it's all gone."

I hit and punched and cried at the injustice of being left by my mother with tubes in my nose and monitors on my chest. After I had no more punch in me, I fell in a heap on the floor.

The rage was out.

I took off my gloves that day and hung them on the back of my bedroom door. I keep them there to remind me that my fighting days are over.

I almost put them back on after what Gleason Beal did. I was dying to hit something.

I looked out the window at the dark street below. Opened my scrapbook and wrote:

Transitional teen seeks whereabouts of true father. No questions asked. No leads too small.

I turned to the back section of the scrapbook where I keep The Dads. Over the years I've cut out pictures of men from magazines that I thought looked like father material. Not guys with rock-star hair or strange clothes—businessmen mostly, all with great smiles. Some of them I got from life insurance ads; they were holding their kids and looking like they'd never leave them. Steadfastness is the best trait for a father, in my opinion, and believe me, I've studied the species. When you're in food service, you see the best and worst of parenting on any given weekend.

I smoothed back my hair, sat Edgar, my stuffed pelican, on the pillow.

Enter fantasy.

Music swells.

"Dad, I need to talk to you about something important."

I picture him instantly putting down the significant stack of papers he's working on. He turns around in his green leather chair. He has a deep, kind voice. "Well, of course, Hope. I always have time for you."

"I know, Dad, that you've been all over the world and you've managed to make those transitions easily because you're the kind of person who doesn't let change throw you, but I'm having some problems doing that here. I'm doing stuff with people, I'm involved and all, but deep down I don't feel like I fit in Wisconsin. I'm more of a big-city person, like you."

I picked up Edgar, hugged him. "I can't seem to get over the fact that you aren't here, Dad. I'm trying to be hopeful, but it's hard. Sometimes I wonder if I should change my name to something that doesn't lug so much responsibility with it. Susan, maybe. Lucy.

"If you could give me some advice right now about my life

and how long it's going to take you to find me, I'd sure appreciate it."

I waited, listening to the soft ticks of my alarm clock.

Sometimes this game works and sometimes it doesn't.

3:14 A.M.

Still awake and emoting.

I took out my Roget's thesaurus, which lists words that have the same meaning. If you're a word person like me, you can't live without one. Say you're trying to get an idea across, like *Gleason Beal is a thief.* You can look up the word "thief" in the thesaurus and come up with a slew of even better slams to help you work out your intense feelings.

Gleason Beal is a . . .

. . . robber.

. . . stealer.

. . . purloiner (I like that one).

. . . larcenist.

. . . pilferer.

. . . poacher.

. . . swindler.

I flipped to the H section.

Hope is . . .

. . . belief.

. . . credence.

. . . faith.

. . . trust.

. . . confidence.

. . . assurance.

I lay on the bed, holding the thesaurus, trying to live up to my name.

I lurched toward dawn. Got to work at 5:00 A.M., a half-hour early (points for me), to set up for the breakfast crowd. Addie had been baking bread since four. I learned years ago not to try to outwork that woman. Braverman wasn't due in until later that morning. No tall presence overshadowing the grill. I kind of missed him.

There's something about diner setup that soothes the soul. Something about making good coffee in a huge urn glistening in fluorescent light, something sweet about filling syrup pitchers and lining them on the back counter like soldiers ready to advance. It gives you courage to face another day.

The doors opened at 6:00 A.M. By seven, we were packed.

In minutes, I got every kind of sitter at the counter. I love watching people sit down. There are ploppers, slammers, sliders, swivelers, and my personal favorite, flutterers, who poise suspended above the seat and move up and down over it before finally lighting.

At the galley window I heard Lou Ellen snarl to someone: "*I* had to drive forty miles with a baby to get this job. That Hope just waltzes in here—no interview—like she owns the place."

Like *I* had a choice in any of this.

I rammed into high gear to show her up.

Stepped over the legs of a burly construction worker that were stretched out in the aisle. Some people do not know how to behave in public. Daphne Kroll, night waitress at the

Humdinger Diner, would just stop dead in front of someone with loose legs and say, "Honey, are you charging a toll, or is passage free today?" Daphne could get away with that because she was middle-aged and built like a walk-in cooler. When you're sixteen, trust me, step over the legs.

At the counter listening to Adam Pulver tell G.T. about his uncle Sid, who is a spin doctor and had helped two congressmen win seats in the last two elections.

"Spin doctor . . ." Flo was clearing plates, listening in like a good waitress should. "You mean one of those fellas who takes what people say and turns it around to mean something else? They give me a headache."

Adam rose defensively. "My uncle is a genius. The last guy he worked for was behind thirty-five points in the polls. Uncle Sid found the button of the district and his candidate *won*."

G.T. sipped his coffee. "What was the button?"

Adam's face got reverent. "Waste disposal. Uncle Sid is coming to visit tomorrow. He says you have one of the most interesting campaigns he's ever heard of, G.T., and he'd like to meet you."

G.T. smiled, but didn't say anything.

Adam lowered his voice. "He's going to be staying with us while his ulcer heals."

Flo piped in, "I don't think G.T. needs a spin doctor."

Adam bolted up. "*Everyone* needs a spin doctor."

Sid Vole, spin doctor supreme, is eating a farmer's breakfast special not exactly for the ulcer sufferer: three eggs scrambled with onions, peppers, and sausage; Addie's life-changing hash browns; a side of buckwheat pancakes with real maple syrup; melon chunks; black coffee. He has a round baby face like Adam and styled, shellacked hair.

He's sitting at the big eight-top surrounded by Adam, G.T., Brice, Jillian, and G.T.'s barber, Slick Bixby, who just said that after thirty-five years of cutting hair, he knows Mulhoney, Wisconsin, like only a man who wields his scissors on the great and the below average can. I'm the waitress—a direct challenge because people keep pulling up chairs to the table and wanting coffee. I'd bring it; then it would dawn on them that they wanted an English muffin; then some orange juice; maybe a fat stack of Addie's brown sugar pecan pancakes that were beginning to catch fire in town. I'm doing my best to make life nice for everyone, but it's not like this is the only table I've got.

Pastor Al B. Hall comes into the diner like a bolt of lightning. That man knows how to make an entrance. G.T. waves him over. I bring his coffee as Sid Vole takes a pill and leans back, arms behind his head.

"It takes a clear vision to win in politics. You clarify that— ram that baby home whenever someone asks you a question—doesn't matter what the question is; doesn't matter who's asking—just find a way to jump into the vision thing and you'll sting like a bee."

G.T. and Slick look at each other. Pastor Hall orders huevos rancheros (Mexican eggs and tortillas with hot sauce)—people with guts order that. I pour more coffee for everyone.

"Basically," Sid Vole explains, "the whole messy game of politics is about trust. Search for leadership in the age of cynicism. The cancer could work for you, G.T. It's a fresh angle. People sense you can feel their pain. The problem is dying. I guess that's always the problem." Sid Vole chuckles. "I think your best shot is to stay above the fray. Be *Mr.* Clean." He looks at G.T.'s shiny head. "We could get you an earring like that genie on the disinfectant cleaner."

G.T. laughs and shakes his head.

"Maybe that's overkill, no pun intended. Millstone's got a big problem with you because you're going to have people's sympathy even if they don't vote your way. If Millstone hits too hard he could demonize himself, which is what you pray for. But you've got to know how to play this trust thing just right."

My head is swimming.

I walk fast to the galley window, call in, "Huevos." Waitresses order in shorthand—saves time. Braverman flips his spatula in the air and nods. I miss the way Morty the cabdriver talked about politics—he'd sit at the counter, pounding his knife, spearing dinner rolls, screaming that politicians were out to get the little guy.

Yuri's cleaning tables like a machine. He looks at me, smiling. "Someday I vote American."

"Me, too, Yuri."

He takes a book from his pocket, *Moving Toward Citizenship*.

He opens the book, points to the word *freedom*. "Best word," he says with feeling.

"The best." I'm grinning as I bring two guys Blistermeyer's Death Sauce for their eggs.

Three women plop next to the big table, saying how they've heard about the wonderful food here.

"Welcome, women."

I hear Sid Vole: "Politics is war—don't ever forget that. In the words of that great military strategist Napoleon Bonaparte, the number-one thing that is going to make this campaign succeed is 'to keep our forces united, to be vulnerable at no point, to bear down with rapidity upon important points'—these are 'the principles which insure victory.' "

Adam is glowing, writing it all down.

The three women order decaf with skim milk; herbal tea with brown sugar; iced tea with a "bendy" straw and a little honey on the side.

Labor intensive. I write the order down, trying to catch snippets.

Slick: "Here's the problem, Sid—people know G.T. as laid-back. I'm not sure hitting so hard is what he's about."

No response from G.T., who is looking out the window at the black hearse that has parked in front of the diner again.

Sid: "That's an old trick. My advice is, find out this mayor's weakest point and send out a strong visual reminder to him and the voters."

Adam half rises in vindication.

G.T. sniffs. "My mother wouldn't have liked that much."

"Mothers aren't usually an asset in politics."

"Mine is."

Huevos up. Swing up to the window, swing back to Al B. Hall, who says, "Bless you," and would I get him a bottle of Satan's Red-Hot Revenge for the eggs?

Sure thing, Pastor.

G.T. gets up without a word, goes out the door, walks right to that hearse, and shakes the driver's hand. Everyone in the Welcome Stairways is standing now, looking out the windows.

Sid Vole whispers, "This is risky. Meeting the enemy."

G.T. opens the hearse's door and motions for the man to come inside. The man doesn't want to, he's all rattled—bullies usually are when you confront them—but G.T. takes him kindly by the arm and leads him up the red welcome stairways, into the diner, and right to the big table. He puts a menu in the thug's hand and says to me, "Now, Hope, you get my friend here whatever he wants for breakfast."

The man says he isn't hungry, really; he has to go, but I sense deep within his thugness that he needs a special meal. So I say, "May I recommend Addie's homemade corned beef hash and fried eggs with a big piece of maple corn bread slathered with salted butter?"

The thug gulps. I have him. He nods, hands me the menu. I doubt he will leave a tip, but this isn't about money.

"Sir, can I get you some coffee, juice?"

"Coffee," he says, warming to my power.

"Coffee it is."

I speed off to the galley, where I'm about to call in the order.

The hash and eggs are already frying.

"I heard," Addie says.

The sweet synergy of food service.

Braverman tosses a cherry tomato in the air and catches it in his mouth.

I bring the thug his coffee as G.T. is saying, "The thing I hate most about dying is how we deny its existence for as long as we can. Nobody knows how long they've got on this earth. And we all need to live our lives just a little bit like the hearse is outside ready to cart us away—make the days count. That doesn't mean living in fear, but we don't have to be dumb bunnies either and take life for granted. I thank you for that reminder, friend. You cruise by with that old thing anytime you want."

The thug looks down at his coffee, grabs the mug with two hands, as several people in the diner start applauding. Then more people start and soon everyone is clapping. I would be clapping, too, except I'm carrying four of Addie's tomato-and-leek breakfast pizzas to table twelve, so I throw back my head and shout, "Yes!" Sid Vole thumps G.T. on the back with political glee. Adam shouts that G.T.'s petition is at the register if anyone wants to sign. People stream up to sign that thing.

Addie dings the bell twice. My signal. I sweep to the galley window; take that thug's plate steaming with everything a human being could hope for in a breakfast. Place it gently in front of him and slip away.

Sometimes you hover and sometimes you let the food do the work.

8

To spin or not to spin.

That was the question.

Everyone, minus Sid Vole, was still gathered at the big table.

"This campaign," snarled Slick Bixby, "doesn't need a spin doctor."

Pastor Hall leaned forward. "I'm not so sure. How many of us understand politics?" No hands were raised. "How many of us have any idea how to get someone elected?"

"We haven't got money for this!" Slick Bixby protested.

G.T. sipped his coffee. "Sid said given what we're trying to do here, he'd lower his rate considerably." He turned to me. "What do you think, Hope?"

Well, I was shocked to be asked, but I knew enough not to shrug. Adults hate it when teenagers do that. "I think it's like working with a brilliant, difficult cook, G.T. You put up with a lot to get the magic."

G.T. slapped the table and said that was exactly right.

Al B. Hall shouted, "Are you paying this young woman enough?"

I smiled extravagantly because I can always use more cash.

"We're ready to order, dear." A woman at the front window booth waved her napkin at me, cutting short my moment in the sun.

Five days passed. Strange days. We'd gotten 227 signatures on the petition and were waiting for the official nod from the Election Board that G.T. was on the ballot. But like Sid Vole said, you never stand still in politics, you keep blazing new trails on the campaign front and looking behind you in case the opposition is trying to steal your wallet.

Politics gripped the town.

Everyone had an opinion about G.T., honesty, disease, and why suddenly the tax assessor's office was closed.

"They're doing something to the dairy's tax records," Braverman shouted.

Working the counter was like hosting one of those angry TV shows where people screamed at each other and no one ever got to finish a thought.

Emotion gripped the kitchen, but it wasn't political. Addie introduced her butterscotch cream pie and marinated flank steak to rave reviews. She was pushing perfection out of that kitchen and refining Braverman in the process.

"My boy, when you're cutting a chicken, you want a clean severing at the bone. You don't want snags or shards breaking off, now do you?"

"No," said Braverman, towering over a raw chicken.

"A chicken is a gift from God, but *only* when it is properly prepared. A badly prepared chicken is a gift to no one."

Braverman nodded grimly.

"And *meatloaf*," Addie cried, "is not to be abused. You don't shove it in a pan with tomato juice and oatmeal. You mold it with care. You mix it with onions and spices and Worcester sauce and form it into a free-standing loaf and *never* put it in a loaf pan. You slather it with barbecue sauce, which caramelizes over the loaf when it cooks."

It was clear Braverman had not spent much time thinking about meatloaf.

I left them alone. Trekked outside to take my break. Sat on a bench in the garden. The sun smiled down on the rows of trees, a stone path curled between them. Nothing overdone, just natural beauty all around. G.T. walked from behind a big tree.

"You had the tour out back?"

I shook my head.

"Well, come on over here and meet my memories."

I walked over; he pulled a few dead leaves off the biggest tree. "I planted this oak twenty-five years ago when I got married. You would have liked my wife, Hope. Gracie was tough like you."

I smiled—a tough one.

He walked over to a smaller tree that had lost most of its pink flowers. "Planted this dogwood four years ago when she died."

I gulped. "I'm sorry . . ."

He picked up a pink flower from the ground. "She managed the diner from bed and the couch upstairs. Did the books, thought up the menus. Gracie'd been sick with rheumatoid arthritis for years, but it didn't stop her." He kept walking. "Those white birches are for the three grocery stores my parents owned. My folks were always half broke from giving food away to people who needed it. This Japanese maple went in the ground eight years ago when Al opened his church."

It had beautiful red leaves. "You must be good friends."

He slapped the bark. "He doesn't walk out on me when I overcook a steak and I don't walk out on him when his sermons get too long."

He knelt down chuckling, scooped up dirt from the ground, let it run through his fingers.

I stood there wondering if he could beat the cancer or if it would beat him.

"Know why I plant trees?"

"No."

"I like thinking they'll be here long after I'm gone. All those fine memories pushing up to the sky."

I thought about all the times I'd written HOPE WAS HERE above dessert cases, bedroom doors, and on boarded-up windows.

A sweet breeze blew, rustling the tree leaves.

"I hope you're here for the longest time possible, G.T."

He smiled so full. He had the kind of smile that took over his face.

Right then the back door creaked open and Adam Pulver slumped toward us in all-out grief.

G.T. stood up. "What is it?"

Adam shook his head like he was lost.

"The Election Board said fifty-five of our names had wrong information." He lowered his head. "G.T., they say you're off the ballot."

"*What?*" I stormed forward.

Adam was close to tears. "I don't know how it happened. We checked every name *three times.*"

G.T. sat quietly at the counter, staring into his full coffee cup.

Adam kept saying he hadn't meant to mess up.

Addie was pained, peering out from the kitchen.

Yuri looked miserably into a bus pan of dirty dishes. "We are all together sad."

Braverman threw his Milwaukee Brewers hat on the floor. "Millstone got to someone at the Election Board!"

Sid Vole ate a toasted pecan roll, hearing everyone out, which surprised me. He popped an ulcer pill, downed it with black coffee. "First lesson in politics. Don't let a locked door stop you. I'd advise a showdown at the Election Board tomorrow morning. It's the only way."

Braverman and I had to work that night and I wasn't in the mood for hassle. Lou Ellen was working, too. Skating on the edge was more like it. She looked like she hadn't slept in a week. Her pale face was drawn. Her hands were shaking. She guzzled her fourth Coke of the evening.

"Are you okay?" I ask.

Her eyes seem almost soft. "No," she says, and starts crying.

"You want to take a break?"

"No." She's crying harder.

"I think it might be a good idea."

The waitress bell. "Flank steaks up," Braverman says.

"That's me, Lou Ellen. I'll be right back."

"My baby's sick, Hope."

I stop. "I'm sorry."

"She's not eating right and the doctor says she's not gaining weight like she should. She's fourteen months old, old enough to be sitting up herself, and she's not doing that either."

"Oh . . ."

The bell again.

Give me a break, Braverman.

"My mom said I must have done something wrong when I was pregnant, but I did everything the doctor said. I swear to God!"

"I believe you."

Two angry dings from the kitchen.

I lead her to the counter to sit down. Run to the galley window. Grab the flank steaks. Braverman barks, "You got something better to do than pick up your order?"

I say nothing. I'm a professional. I remind myself that cooks work all day in hot enclosed places and this alters their brains. Deliver the flank steaks as Lou Ellen breaks down crying by the dessert case. I never thought of her having such a trial.

That's when the front door opens and into my life pours an army of laughing, boisterous men who announce they're all from the Elks Lodge and boy are they hungry.

They fill the eight window booths.

In seconds, I'm in the weeds.

I ram into fourth gear.

Run past Lou Ellen, who's a basket case. Tell her I'll be with her in a minute. Give everyone menus. Calmly tell the Elks that I'm going to get to them one at a time, I swear.

"This herd's not going anywhere, little lady," an old Elk says, which breaks the others up. I laugh, too, although inside I'm dying.

I break free, rush to Lou Ellen, who says, "I'm too upset to work, Hope. I don't mean to leave you flat. I just don't think..." She's crying again.

I grab her hand. "Go home."

My head's spinning with sick babies and election boards. Six more Elks take the corner booth. The herd is growing.

I run to the kitchen, raise my finger to Braverman. "I've got four dozen hungry Elks out there that could start a stampede at any minute. Don't push my buttons, Braverman."

"Do they all have antlers?"

"They all have menus. *Get ready.*"

He swings into action.

I shout, *"Yuri, I'm in the weeds!"*

Yuri rushes out from the supply closet, confused.

"Explain, please ... weeds."

"Lines like Russia!"

"I help for you!"

I burst from the kitchen, Warrior Waitress, stand by those booths, yucking it up at bad jokes.

How many elks does it take to change a lightbulb?

None. They can see in the dark.

Flash my pearly whites at them and they grin back.

To make it in the food biz you'd better know about feeding animals.

"Welcome, men." Yuri's running with water and setups. "You come ... from afar?"

"Just down the street," the head Elk says.

I've faced hungry herds before. If a lot of them order the same thing, it'll be easier on me and Braverman.

"Just to let you know we've got a delicious pork-chop sandwich and a meatloaf special that is famous up and down the East Coast."

That gets them. Meat men order fast.

Fourteen pork chops; twenty-one meatloaves. Six burger specials. Seven bowls of chili.

But there's always a turkey.

He was big with an attitude. "I need *my* order fast," he informs me, checking his watch. No eye contact.

"What did you order, sir?"

"I just told you."

I take a deep breath. I've just taken dozens of orders. "You're going to have to give me a little hint ..."

"Begins with P," he says.

Pig, I think, pushing down anger. "Could that be *pork,* sir?"

I don't wait for his answer. That's what he's getting.

I race to the galley. Call in the orders. "And fire me one pork pronto for a bozo."

"It's going to get crazy in here now!" Braverman shouts, moving like a machine.

Serving salads, tossing rolls in baskets. Keep focused, keep the smile. Everyone's talking between booths, so I play the room like my mom taught me.

"How many want coffee?"

A sea of hands.

"I'm going to make an extra pot. Would the most caffeine needy raise your hands higher?"

Good laughs.

I pour, grinning. Deliver Bozo Man's pork-chop sandwich. He doesn't say thank you.

Ding. Ding.

Six plates layered on my left arm. I make the trip again and again from the kitchen.

"Is everybody having a good time?" I shout.

Oh yeah, we sure are!

"More coffee?"

Oh yeah.

And I move through it.

I always do.

Braverman doesn't mess up once either. Yuri gets Bus Man of the Year.

Finally, the herd leaves. I pick up my excellent tips and wave good-bye like a frontier woman in an old Western.

I give Yuri a big tip. Waitresses always tip bus people at the end of the shift.

I clean the tables and the counter; fill ketchups, mustards. Wipe down the coffee urns. Walk back into the kitchen.

Braverman is chopping onions. He has a lighted candle that casts a weird shadow by the chopping block. His big hands move slow compared with Addie's. He doesn't say anything; I don't either. I wonder where he lives and how he feels about not going to college.

Braverman looks at his onion. "You did a good job tonight, Hope."

"So did you."

Chop, chop. "Look, I'm sorry I yelled at you about the flank steaks."

I never once had a cook apologize. "It's okay, Braverman. It's been a hard day."

"You look tired. I'll lock up."

I can hardly keep my eyes open. "I'll let you."

9

Election Board desk, 9:00 A.M.

Present: G.T., Braverman, Adam, Sid Vole, Brice, Jillian, Pastor Hall, and me. We were all wearing red-and-blue campaign buttons—STOOP FOR MAYOR was a little off-center. Adam had stayed up late making them with the button machine he had gotten for his birthday. He *knew* they were off-center and he didn't want to hear any comments because we were a campaign *without* T-shirts, bumper stickers, or decent giveaways of any kind. This was it, and we'd better be grateful.

I was working hard to be grateful as the Election Board administrator looked past the buttons and refused to smile at several key moments.

When Sid Vole told her that he knew the governor.

When Adam told her he had been an intern in this very office during spring break and being back was just like coming home.

She showed us the fifty-five names that were a problem—all had the wrong addresses.

Braverman threw his hands up. "That's impossible."

G.T. asked her how, in her opinion, this could have happened.

"Inexperience," she barked, which caused Adam and Sid Vole to turn maroon.

"I wonder," G.T. continued, "if something else happened. Was there ever a mistake on the Election Board listings? A series of mistakes?"

"No," she snapped.

"That's certainly been known to happen," Sid Vole observed.

"Not here," she said sharply.

G.T. stepped forward. "Ma'am, I don't know if you can do it, but I've come to ask the Election Board to give us a little more time. I can promise you that—"

She shuffled the papers on her desk. "I can't do that, Mr. Stoop. Rules are rules."

G.T. bowed his head sadly. "I appreciate you hearing me out."

It was over.

We stood there frozen.

That's when Pastor Hall marched up smiling at that administrator, energy pouring off him. "You know what I love about the Lord?" he asked her.

That startled woman shook her head.

Al B. Hall grinned deep. "That his mercies are new every morning. He always gives a second chance."

The woman fidgeted in her chair.

"Always," Al B. Hall continued, pointing right at her. "Even if we imperfect beings mess up again and again and do things that we'll regret for *years* to come. The Lord is there understanding our weakness, reaching out his kind, *forgiving* hand and saying, 'Let me help you change your ways. Let me give you my love for people. Let me fill you with my ...' " he leaned forward, " *'mercy.'* " He clapped his hands. "And isn't it a fine thing to know that right now God Almighty is looking down at us wanting to lead us in the way that is best? *Doesn't that make you want to shout hallelujah?*"

"Hallelujah," said Braverman and Adam.

The Election Board administrator grabbed her necklace.

"I ... I suppose ... I could ..." She stopped short.

Pastor Hall helped her out. *"Reconsider."*

"I ... could give you ... well ... until five today."

Yes!

"God bless you!" Pastor Hall shook her pudgy hand. "Doesn't it feel good to do the Lord's work?"

We decided not to wait for her answer and ran out the door tripping over each other in a great show of uncoordination, despite our buttons.

"Get as many extra names as you can," Sid Vole shouted, "and check every one against the master list. We take this hill at all costs!" He turned to Al B. Hall. "Pastor, you know how to spin."

Pastor Hall cocked his bush hat and grinned.

We spread out like detectives trying to find an escaped convict.

Farmer's Market. Bustling with people. Addie was with me, spitting mad about G.T.'s Election Board hassle; browbeating the local growers in her search for proper tomatoes and meaningful garlic.

I'd gotten one signature in an hour from Deputy Babcock, but one signature wasn't going to help much. Too many people there were from other towns and couldn't vote in our district. I walked to the parking lot to accost newcomers.

Two guys shuffled toward me. They looked old enough to vote, but they didn't look like they'd showered. They were poking each other, laughing too hard. I moved off.

Too late.

"Ohhhh," said one. "She don't like us."

One raced in front of me, the other one got behind me.

They looked me up and down. "But we like her." The tall one moved in close. "You got a boyfriend?"

I put my hand up. "Get away from me."

They were blocking my path. I tried to get past them: couldn't. There was no one else around.

"I'd like to be your boyfriend."

Their leering faces made me sick. One of them grabbed my petition, the other pointed at my STOOP button and said I was stupid to be doing what I was doing. I told him to back off; G.T. was a good man. The tall one grabbed my arm, started pulling me toward him. Fear shot through me. I bent over low like I'd learned in boxing.

"Help!" I yelled. *"Help!"*

"Now why'd you go do that?" I could smell his rancid breath.

I saw Deputy Babcock running toward me. Addie was sprinting behind her.

That's why.

"What's going on here?" Deputy Babcock shouted.

"Nuthin'," said one of the guys, dropping the petition on the ground. He had stained brown teeth.

I broke free. "They wouldn't let me pass. They took my petition." I pointed to the tall one. "He was grabbing my arm."

Deputy Babcock, hand on her gun, stared them down. "That doesn't sound like nothing to me."

"Well . . ." the taller one mumbled. "You don't come from these parts, *ma'am*." He didn't look at her when he said it. His voice showed his disrespect.

A moron and a racist. The two sure go together.

Deputy Babcock didn't flinch. "That's right. I come from a real big city where we call this *harassment*." She said to me, "Are you all right?"

"Yeah." I was shaking.

"I'll get your statement later."

She took her gun from her holster, motioned those creeps toward her squad car. "You have the right to remain silent, *gentlemen*."

I'd never heard anyone say that except on television.

"We didn't do nuthin'!"

"Duly noted." She marched those lowlifes forward, reading them their rights.

Addie was by my side now. "You all right?"

I picked up the petition with shaking hands. "I think so."

"Good Lord," she wailed, "I thought small towns were safe."

A farmer was next to us now. "They're bad ones. The whole family of Carbingers is. Five boys, each one worse than the next. They live on the edge of town. Try to stay away from them."

I made it my life goal to do just that.

An old woman walked slowly up to me, handed me a beautiful orange flower with a long stem.

"I'm Mavis Pettibone." She had a gravelly voice. "G.T. probably knows what he's in for. I'm not sure you do. Put this daylily in water in a sunny place and watch what happens. Whatever you do to help his campaign—*whatever* happens, girl—you remember the power of the light."

I stood there gripping the flower.

I poured water in a tall, thin vase, plopped the daylily in, and placed it near our kitchen window. I didn't hold out much hope for this flower. It looked withered, closed, and utterly dead.

I ran downstairs to help Flo through the dinner rush. Addie's tamale pie with cornmeal pastry was selling like lotto tickets.

Adam strutted into the diner and gave the news.

They made it to the Election Board at 4:58.

G.T. was officially on the ballot.

I did a little dance and Flo joined me.

Braverman flipped his spatula high in the air and caught it behind his back.

When hope gets released in a place, all kinds of things are possible.

The next morning, Mrs. Pettibone's daylily stood tall in that vase, fully opened—soaking up the goodness of the light.

"We've got ourselves an official horse race now, G.T."

Eli Millstone walked to the counter to shake G.T.'s hand. He had a photographer with him who took a picture of the handshake.

Millstone held up a campaign poster of himself. "I don't suppose you'll be wanting to put this up in your front window by any chance, will you, G.T.?" He smiled so the photographer could get a shot of him being folksy.

G.T. gave him a menu and said he'd buy him breakfast.

"You're not trying to buy me off, are you, G.T.? That's taking unfair advantage." He said this loud.

"I'm glad you brought that up, Eli. Buying people off is one of the things we need to talk about in this campaign."

Flo almost dropped her coffeepot.

"Those are fighting words, G.T., especially from a man in *your* condition."

G.T. put his hands in his pockets. "Eli, has your relationship with the Real Fresh Dairy compromised the interests of this town?"

The whole place went quiet.

"That dairy," Millstone sputtered, "is the biggest thing that ever happened to this town!"

"It's blocks long. I'll give you that."

A loud whistle from the kitchen.

The photographer was clicking away. Millstone screamed, *"Stop that!"*

Down went the Nikon.

Up came the bull.

Millstone straightened his shoulders; found the old smile; looked into the eyes of all those registered voters.

"Good people of Mulhoney, I can assure you that I have always worked to protect your interests. I have dedicated myself to bringing a better life to every man, woman, and child in this town."

He adjusted his expensive gold watch; the photographer clicked off a few shots.

"Mr. Mayor." Cecelia Culpepper rose from her seat at the counter. "When will you be releasing the names of your campaign contributors?"

His eyes flashed. "You'll have to talk to my office about that."

He gave a meaningful salute to the voters and was halfway out the door when Cecelia Culpepper shouted, "No one's returned my calls."

Millstone kept on walking.

10

Lou Ellen's baby, Anastasia, was lying in the portable playpen that had been set up in the back office that Adam had turned into Campaign Central. Red, white, and blue streamers curled across the ceiling; small American flags stood on the desk, a computer printout of Adam's first-draft campaign slogan was taped to the wall—STOOP FOR MAYOR—A MAN FOR ALL SEASONS AND ALL REASONS. It needed work.

Lou Ellen was looking at Anastasia, who wasn't playing with any of her toys.

"The doctor says she's got development problems." Lou Ellen said it defensively. "I've got to watch her for a few weeks because they can't do it right at day care and my mom can't look after her on account of her job. G.T. said I could bring her here."

"It's real good you did," Flo said reassuringly.

We were going to take turns watching Anastasia so Lou Ellen could work. She kept saying the baby would be fine, we didn't have to put ourselves out.

"Stop that, honey," Flo directed. "Let us help you through this."

Lou Ellen went stiff.

Adam was up first to the playpen. He studied the toys, lifted the busy box, held it in front of Anastasia, pushed down the little orange lever that made a clicking sound. "See, Anastasia, that's how you vote for G.T. You try." She didn't.

"She can't do much!" Lou Ellen shouted. Her face was tight with emotion. I tried to reach for her hand, but she backed out the door fast and ran off.

"Now this is how you drive to the polling place." Adam put Anastasia's tiny hands on a little wheel.

But Anastasia didn't respond.

A volunteer fireman's barbecue, two church socials, and a meeting of the Beautification Committee of Greater Mulhoney. G.T. was on fire, burning up the campaign trail. Giving speeches whenever he was asked.

Sid Vole had definite rules for writing speeches.

"Hit with two ideas, three at most. Tell them what you're going to say; say it; then tell them what you said."

But G.T. stood firm. "I don't believe in writing speeches, Sid. My Quaker roots go too deep. I'm trusting God to give me the right words when I need them."

Sid Vole's face contorted like he'd heard a violin played off-key.

His ulcer got worse when G.T. addressed the Rotary Club.

"You should know that if you elect me mayor I won't spend

any time trying to get your votes for the next election. I won't be feathering my nest for my retirement. Chances are I won't be around for any of that. I will roll up my sleeves and ask you to do the same."

Sid Vole took G.T. aside. "We need to give you an air of permanence with the voters. Like the sun who will always be in the sky."

G.T. laughed. "I think I'm more like a passing cloud, Sid."

June blended into July.

Adam came up with a new campaign slogan.

STOOP FOR MAYOR:

HE'LL DIE TRYING TO MAKE THINGS BETTER.

Sid Vole said it was the perfect spin: admit we have a problem, redefine the problem to make it a positive. He took a little plastic top out of his pocket and spun it on the table. Adam had a top, too, but when he spun his it fell to the floor.

In the midst of this, I got a seven-page letter with cheesy New York postcards from Harrison and Miriam talking about how much they missed me. I read it five times, put the pictures around the mirror in my room.

Memories crashed over me.

Harrison, Miriam, and me going to poetry readings at bookstores (key entertainment—they were free).

There was that last poet we heard before I moved—the one with the scraggly beard and the torn T-shirt.

"I am the zebra without stripes," he read, "shouting from the subways of the city." Emotional pause. "But you know me."

"What did that mean?" I asked when it was over.

Miriam munched a hazelnut biscotti. "He's on drugs."

"It *means*," Harrison explained, "he's lost his identity like a zebra losing its stripes. He's become a person without . . . without the marks of what he used to be. But deep inside the subway of his soul he knows who he is. We know . . . because he is us. He shouts for us all."

Harrison can pull meaning from a stone. Both of his parents are English teachers.

"If he shouts too loud in the subway he'll get arrested," Miriam added.

I wrote them back using calligraphy lettering for extra drama.

First, guys, The Good: I'm working on a political campaign with a man who should probably be running for governor or president for all the good he could bring to people's lives.

The Bad: There are no tall buildings—anywhere. Food-wise, except for Addie, think Dark Ages. No Thai, dim sum, jerk chicken. No museums either.

The Oblique: There's this guy I work with and I'm trying to figure him out.

I put down my pen.

I didn't know how to tell them how much I missed them. Couldn't let them know how hard it is for me to write to people I don't think I'll ever see again. Elaine in Denver. Marla in St. Louis. Josie, Jake, and Jenny in Detroit. I used to promise people that we'd be back to visit, but I stopped doing that.

We don't go back in this family, we just keep moving forward.

I am the zebra without stripes shouting from the U-Haul trailer.

Braverman's ten-year-old twin sisters, Heidi and Hannah, were in the back office playing with Anastasia, who wasn't interested in any of their games. The twins had rosy Wisconsin cheeks and dark braids. Braverman was making them laugh by juggling three new potatoes. Anastasia was not a potato person.

Braverman looped a potato under his leg and grinned at me. He had excellent teeth, healthy gums. That speaks volumes about a person.

I radiated back.

Sid Vole was at the big desk: Not amused.

It probably didn't help that his ulcer wasn't healing. It really didn't help that his doctor had taken him off caffeine, which sure slowed his spin.

Adam, Brice, and Jillian walked in for the meeting.

"Listen up," Sid Vole said. He was yawning so hard we all started yawning, too. "Every successful campaign has one thing in common. The ability to multiply. There are six of us in this room. Six of us each need to go tell ten other people why they should support G.T. Then those people need to find ten more. You get the picture." He put his head on the desk.

"We need to spread like a virus," Adam shouted.

Sid Vole looked up briefly. "Call it something else on the street."

We called it Students for Stoop and we were revved for spreading the word.

"Assume nothing!" Adam shouted. "Ask people the critical question. Will they vote for G.T.? Call your neighbors. Tell your friends. Bother your parents!"

"Can someone else bother my dad?" Brice pleaded. "He's pretty mad since I crashed his Honda into that beer truck."

"Last time it was a Federal Express truck," Jillian whispered to me.

Jillian and I were becoming good friends. She had a passionate relationship with her computer, which connected her to the outside world. She didn't expect life to be easy either, and avoided giggliness, which I really appreciated. She had one major flaw—an unshakable belief that someday Adam Pulver would be president.

"Of the United States?" I asked, aghast.

"I'm telling you, Hope, kids like Adam are born with the dream. Remember the things he does so that years from now when the media wants to talk to people who knew him when, you'll be ready."

"You're going to vote for G.T., aren't you, Addie?"

It was probably the wrong time to ask, since she had just smeared cold cream all over her face. She slapped a steaming towel on her face and shuddered. I hadn't seen her do this for ages.

"G. T. Stoop's being a stubborn fool and I can't believe that a human being with his potential is ignoring his health needs in such a fashion!"

I looked at the "Voter Reality" sheet that Adam had made up. It had four boxes to choose from after asking the CQ (critical question).

YES

NO

MAYBE

ABANDON HOPE

I didn't like my name being used like that.

"But you're going to vote for him, right, Addie?"

Addie held the towel tight across her face, breathing deeply. "Well, of course I am."

I checked *YES*. Stubborn adults stick together.

"Can you help us on the campaign?"

"I've been baking extra and sending it to the back office every day."

In the space marked *How This Person Can Help the Campaign*, I wrote: *Already a major food source.*

A knock on the front door. I walked down the hall to answer it.

Jillian was standing there holding her laptop.

"I'm too humble to say I'm a genius, Hope, but you've got to see this."

Students for Stoop

It was huge across the computer screen. Jillian scrolled down. Several headings: *The Man, The Message, The Meaning, How You Can Get Involved.*

"You did this?" I asked.

"Every gorgeous word." Jillian clicked on *Students for Stoop* and it morphed into bouncing letters. "And the soundtrack please." She clicked again; rock music started playing.

"Jillian, that's amazing."

She was grinning and typing. "Okay, here's how they contact us. I'm going to send mail out to kids at the high school to tell everyone what we're doing." Click. Up on the screen came *What teens are saying about G. T. Stoop and why you should listen.* "I need a major quote from you, Hope. We'll put it right here. Say something instantly fabulous."

"Can I think about it?"

"Time's up. Why do you think G.T. should be mayor?"

"Because he's totally honest, completely fair, and he cares about everyone's welfare."

Jillian typed that in.

"Wait a minute—"

"No, it's good. Braverman said G.T. would bring honor and humility to the office." She looked straight at me. "Braverman's going to edit a Students for Stoop newsletter to promote G.T."

"That's nice."

She kept looking.

"What?" I demanded.

"Hope, I have to say it. You and Braverman would be perfect together."

My face got hot.

"I mean," Jillian gushed, "you have this *force* connecting you. It's under the surface, but it runs deep."

I looked out the window, trying to appear casual.

Anyone who's spent any time in food service knows the peril.

"I don't date people I work with, Jillian. It's disaster."

My heart was thub-dubbing as I recited my mother's Number One Cardinal Rule of Waitress Survival—DO NOT, UNDER ANY CIRCUMSTANCES, DATE THE COOK. Mom had been fired twice for doing this. "Cooks tend to move from thing to thing quickly," Mom explained. "A waitress who dates the cook *always* gets burned." She wrote that in her last Christmas letter.

"But if you didn't work with him, Hope—"

I didn't tell her the truth—that, just maybe, I'd like to go out with him, but I hadn't let myself go there. I'd only had one boyfriend, Bobby Ray Goshen from Pensacola, but he was part-time. He cheated on me.

"I don't live in what-ifs, Jillian. I go with what's on the menu." This wasn't entirely true.

"You're impossible."

"I try."

She ate one of Addie's serious double fudge brownies that connect people instantly and told me that Braverman needed someone stalwart like me because his last girlfriend dumped him before she went off to college.

"He's a good guy, Hope. He's staying home to help support his mom and sisters. His dad walked out on the family. His mom had an operation and didn't have health insurance, and the bills are pretty rough. That's why he hasn't gone to college yet. He was editor of the high school paper. He was going to major in journalism."

"How do you know all this?"

"In small towns everyone knows everything." Jillian closed her computer. "You *know* he cares for you."

My heart did a back flip.

I went down to the diner to observe Braverman to see if this was true.

"So, Braverman, how's it going?"

"Okay." He was in the kitchen slicing carrots, not acting like he cared for anyone in particular.

"That was a really good pork-chop sandwich you made for my customer at table three earlier. He went on and on about it." I attempted a twinkling laugh. It came out dumb.

"Good." His right eyebrow moved slightly, his jaw tightened. He walked into the supply closet leaving me there.

I reported back to Jillian.

"Like all males, Hope, he has a code that has to be deciphered."

"What's the code?"

"I have no idea. But it's probably weirder than hieroglyphics."

Every day teenagers were coming in to volunteer for G.T.'s campaign, and we knew what to do with them.

Tell ten friends why you support G. T. Stoop and ask them to join you.

Make sure that people are registered to vote for G.T.

Write a letter to the Mulhoney Messenger *telling why you support G.T.'s election.*

Cecelia Culpepper published the letters and an editorial of her own demanding the opening of the tax assessor's office and insisting the mayor release proof that the dairy paid its local taxes.

"We are conducting an internal investigation," said the mayor in response. "The assessor's office will be closed to the public until the investigation is completed."

"Not good enough," Braverman fumed when he read it.

Back at the diner, G.T. was driving himself too hard. Twice I'd seen him steady himself against a wall when he was walking.

Once I saw the color drain from his face when he was

cornered by an irritated representative from Friends of Wildlife who said she could personally assure him of twenty-four votes, but he was going to have to "play ball with the animals."

Sid Vole yawned, still in his decaffeinated state, and studied G.T.'s pale face. "We need to get you in front of people looking strong. Give a thumbs-up sign whenever you can. Voters love that."

G.T. shook his head. "Let's show the people what they're really getting, Sid."

You could feel the campaign heat build. Addie said it was like turning up the flame and quick-frying zucchini that could go from perfection to mush in a matter of seconds.

People were coming into the diner every day just to see what she had on the menu. A man laughed with pure joy yesterday after he'd finished his second bowl of split pea soup brimming with fat ham chunks and garlic butter croutons. That man was dining alone. I saw a marriage proposal take place at table nine. The first thing that happy woman said was, "Harold, it's taken you seven years to ask me. Why now?"

Harold looked at his half-eaten plate of brisket piled with caramelized onions and said he wasn't quite sure, something had come over him.

Addie had a mandate now. She raised a whisk and pointed it at Braverman.

"Now I believe that the way to anyone's heart is through their stomach, and, my boy, I'm here to tell you, we are in the heart business. We're going to reach deep past the menu and into the emotional power of food because a person comes back to a restaurant again and again for one reason only—to feed their soul."

She chopped an onion fast, weeping as the aroma hit her eyes.

Braverman said, "If you light a candle near the chopped onion it takes away the eye sting—that's what I do."

Addie wiped her face and said that weeping just added more passion to the menu.

But she and G.T. were having trouble getting used to each other's ways. Flo said it was like watching two dogs mark off their boundary lines in a field.

The worst face-off was when Addie was trying out a new recipe called Big-Hearted Stew, which had veal and sausage in a tomato-garlic sauce with peas and sautéed onions. She thought she'd used too many onions. G.T. had a bowl of it and said it was perfect, just perfect. Addie said that she was just beginning to reach perfection in this kitchen and she assured him there was a whole lot more to look forward to.

"This is the best cooking this town has seen. And, Lord, people are happy when they leave. You're too hard on yourself, Addie."

"I'm hard on myself because that's the only way food is elevated."

"Maybe you'd have more fun if you backed off a bit."

I tried to signal G.T. that this was the wrong thing to say. Addie's definition of having fun is worrying herself silly over a recipe. She'd reached her fun apex with this veal stew.

Addie snarled, "G.T., there's too much onion in this dish

and I'm not going to serve it until I've got it right. I'm putting something else on the dinner menu."

G.T. said he'd already written out the specials page for the menu for tomorrow and he'd rather not do it again.

"I'll do it then," Addie half shouted, and grabbed a pen and paper and started printing.

"Addie, that's plain wasteful. We can't afford to be throwing out perfectly good food."

Addie looked away. I prayed to God she'd hold it together.

But everything was unraveling.

Four burglaries occurred in town in the same humid, rainy week. One of them was at Adam's house.

"They pulled everything out of the drawers in my room," he cried. "They took my mom's antique clock. They took the stereo and the TV and my dad's campaign button collection that went all the way back to Teddy Roosevelt!" He stared off, shaken.

My hands turned to fists.

"When they come into your house, it's like . . . it's so personal." He was fighting tears. I put my hand on his shoulder.

Deputy Babcock said it seemed like the work of the same person, maybe two people working together.

"Not real swift ones either," she commented, drinking her second cup of coffee at the counter. "They were messy jobs. Whoever it was, though, knew people's patterns—when they'd be home, gone to work. Interesting that whoever it was only burglarized the houses of people who signed G.T.'s petition—or who worked with the campaign."

She adjusted her shoulder holster with the very real pistol. Flo told me that Deputy Babcock used to be a police detective in Minneapolis and moved to Mulhoney to take care of her mother, who lived here and couldn't get around by herself anymore.

"Brenda's got connections way up the pole," Flo told me. "Sheriff Greebs isn't too happy about that."

"Better get the word out," Deputy Babcock said to me and Flo. "Batten down the hatches."

Batten (from Webster's): *A thin narrow strip of lumber used especially to seal or reinforce a joint.*

Hatch: *An opening in the deck of a ship or in the floor or roof of a building.*

"I'd like to know what's being done to find those burglars!" G.T. shouted from the steps of Town Hall after Millstone refused to meet with him about the robberies.

"Sheriff Greebs is conducting a thorough investigation," said a spokesperson for the mayor. "We have no further comments."

"Well, I do," G.T. shot back. "Give the mayor a message for me. Tell him that lies and dirty tricks never win in the long run. Tell him that fear is no way to govern people. He can refuse to meet with me from now until Election Day, but *I will not be silent!*"

Cecelia Culpepper printed it word for word in the *Mulhoney Messenger.*

*   *   *

The next day the Real Fresh Dairy canceled all their advertising with that paper. A few other small businesses pulled their ads, too.

"That's going to hurt Cecelia financially," G.T. said to me. "The dairy was her biggest advertiser. She's had to run that paper on a shoestring since her husband died. My Lord, what we human beings do to each other in the name of politics."

We were out back by the flowering trees. G.T. was holding Anastasia, telling her how he'd prune back the branches so the lush leaves could grow. He told her a story about the mustard seed that was one of the smallest seeds in the tree family, but it turned into one of the mightiest. G.T. said you just never know what can happen when you start planting little seeds.

I went back in the diner to work. Lou Ellen was delivering orders and watching G.T. and Anastasia out the window. She was a pure mess of feelings—running herself ragged trying to work and take care of her child. I wanted to help.

"Lou Ellen, you want me to take table twelve so you can go out and—"

"I need the money, Hope."

"I wasn't doing it for the tip."

"I don't need charity, okay?"

"Lou Ellen, if I can do anything to help like baby-sit, whatever, just ask."

She looked down. "That's real sweet of you. Everyone here's doing so much for me. G.T. said Anastasia could stay here as long as I need." She gripped her order book. "I'm not used to people helping. Except for my mom."

I nodded. "It's good you've got her."

Her face just caved in. I grabbed her limp hand.

She was looking out the window at G.T., who was trying to get Anastasia to touch the flowers on the trees. He put her little hand on the leaves, but it just fell back to her side.

"I named her Anastasia because it was a really big name and I wanted her to do something big in the world. I don't know if she'll ever be able to do much of anything." A tear went down Lou Ellen's cheek. "She doesn't have a daddy either."

Poor kid.

"Neither do I," I said. "Some things you learn to work around."

Lou Ellen looked sympathetic. "Where's yours?"

"I don't know. Where's hers?"

"I don't know either."

I smiled. "Maybe it's some kind of virus."

"Yeah." She half laughed. "The jerk virus."

A man in her station signaled for his check. Lou Ellen steadied herself and wrote it up.

"I think you're real brave," I told her, and for a minute her whole face lit up. She was real pretty when the light went on inside.

"It is with great joy and honor that I announce my support for Eli Millstone, the only man for Mulhoney!" Cranston Broom, president of the Real Fresh Dairy, shouted this into a microphone at his factory as a sea of dairy workers applauded and cheered and several dairy workers draped a Millstone banner across the entrance to the building. "Every dairy truck you see will proudly bear a VOTE FOR ELI poster. That's how committed we are to this mayor."

Braverman, Adam, and I were across the street watching. Braverman's face looked rigid. He sipped the last of his coffee; crushed the Styrofoam cup in his hand.

Braverman was becoming Caffeine Man. In his spare time he worked on the Students for Stoop newsletter and wrote articles for the *Mulhoney Messenger* about the campaign that never got published. Cecelia Culpepper told Braverman that his articles sounded more like editorials. He needed to report the facts, be a "dispassionate observer of the political scene." Braverman said that anyone who was dispassionate about this election was brain-dead.

I was getting worried about him.

"That young man's got a deep relationship with G.T.," Flo explained to me. "It's killing him to hear the things Eli Millstone is saying."

It was killing all of us.

Now, I don't think G. T. Stoop means to be doing this town any harm, but I believe we need to let him know that running for mayor with no experience and leukemia is making a travesty out of the office and is insulting the voters. We all have to understand that this man is not only sick, he's deluded. Every one of his accusations is bosh.

But G.T. went for broke and challenged the people: "Eli's been going around telling you that everything I've said was false. Either I'm the biggest barefaced liar you've ever met or I'm not. You've got to decide."

Braverman started following Millstone's campaign everywhere after that, asking, "What about it, Mr. Mayor? Is G. T. Stoop the biggest barefaced liar we've ever met, or are you?"

The last hour on my shift and it had truly been one of those days.

Everything went wrong in the kitchen, my orders were backed up, I had hungry people glaring at me like I was personally responsible for their starvation.

At the galley window. "I ordered that tortellini sausage soup *twenty minutes ago, Braverman!*"

He slammed a pan. "It was ten minutes ago."

Oh, please!

I had a table full of gimmes ("Gimme water, gimme ketchup"). Mrs. Scarlotti was perched at the counter trying to set me up with her nephew Lewis.

"A nice, thoughtful boy," she said. "Wouldn't hurt a fly."

That means spineless in Brooklyn.

I delivered the world's best chef's salad with crumbled bacon and a large bowl of Too-Good Chili to the people on table seventeen who could see how busy I was and kept telling me not to rush.

Brenda Babcock was sitting at the counter drinking iced coffee. She was in street clothes today—white pants and a bright flowered shirt—she didn't look like she crushed bad guys under her heel in that outfit.

I placed a slice of Addie's fresh coconut layer cake in front of her. That's when we heard the bloodcurdling scream.

"Oh God! Oh God!" The pretty woman on table seventeen shrieked it, covering her face.

I ran over. The man with her looked furiously at me. *"There's half a dead mouse in my wife's salad!"*

This had to be a joke.

The restaurant went silent.

Deputy Babcock was there next to me.

I looked in the salad bowl—saw the top half of a dead, gross rodent, mouth open, covered with Roquefort dressing.

Lou Ellen screamed.

I backed away.

The man stood up. "This is the most disgusting thing I've ever seen!"

He took his soupspoon and held that thing up for everyone to see.

Wails of disgust and disbelief.

Braverman ran to help me from the kitchen. He looked in the bowl, stunned.

"I want to go!" the pretty woman cried. "I might have touched it. Oh, my God! It might be crawling with disease!"

Customers are beginning to gather around us.

"It's really a mouse."

"Don't look, Bobby."

"Inexcusable."

"Sir," I began, "there has never been anything like—"

"We'd heard this was a good, clean place," the man snarled. "Believe me, you'll hear from our lawyer!"

Braverman took the salad bowl. "I don't know how—"

The man took it back. "I need that as evidence."

Brenda Babcock whipped out her deputy's license. "I'll be taking it as evidence. We'll keep it real safe for you and your attorney." She wrote something out on her official deputy pad. "If you'll just sign here."

Suddenly that sweet couple got nervous.

"What . . . do you want us to sign?"

"This just says you found the mouse in your salad."

The woman backed off. "I . . . I don't know if we should sign anything."

"Have you ever seen that mouse before?" Brenda Babcock asked. "Prior to it being in your salad?"

The woman looked down. "How . . . could I have seen it before?"

"Have you, sir?"

"Of course not."

"Then would you sign here, please?"

The couple looked strangely at each other.

No one spoke.

Then a nervous smile. "I think, officer," said the man, "we'd just like to forget the whole thing."

"You will not be pressing charges, then?"

"No," they said together.

"May I see some identification, please?"

"Why," asked the man, "would you want to see that?"

"Because I maintain the peace in this town."

Hard to argue with that.

They took out their driver's licenses. Deputy Babcock wrote down the information.

The woman gulped. "What are you going to do with the mouse?"

"I'm going to have the crime lab check it."

"For what?"

"How long it's been dead. Is it native to these parts. I see you're from Michigan."

"We're traveling through," the man offered quietly.

She handed their licenses back to them. "Enjoy your stay."

The man put a twenty on the table and they walked quickly out the door.

Deputy Babcock turned and addressed the diners. "Go back to your meal, folks. I think we had some visitors who were trying to shut this establishment down."

A collective gasp.

And Deputy Brenda Babcock, crime-fighting ace, raised a humble hand like it was no big deal that she'd just saved the Welcome Stairways from scandal, asked me to keep her cake for later, and marched out the door holding that salad bowl that was sure to reveal major mouse tampering and God knows what else.

12

G.T. and I were in his truck heading off to a day of political campaigning. He'd asked me to come along and be his right-hand person. I couldn't have been more proud.

I checked the schedule that Adam had put together. How he expected two human beings to accomplish all this was beyond me.

"G.T., this is going to be a beast. In eight hours we're supposed to stop at a cheese factory and talk to the workers, hit the commuter train terminal and pass out literature. Meet with leaders of the Small Businessman's Association for lunch. Speak to a parents' meeting about overcrowding in the kindergarten. Go to the Tick Tock Clock Shop for a coffee in your honor. Stop by a bingo game at BVMRCC. I don't even know what that is."

He chuckled. "Blessed Virgin Mary Roman Catholic Church."

I shook my head. Some things shouldn't be abbreviated.

"And Adam made up a list, G.T., of the people who have

contributed to your campaign so far and what they gave. He said we should go over it."

G.T. shook his head. "I never want to see that list."

"Sorry . . ." I put the paper away.

"You can get so messed up learning who gave what and how much that it'll change your opinion of people."

I'd peeked at the list earlier. The biggest contributor was Slick Bixby; the cheapest was Mrs. Scarlotti of Scarlotti's World of Cheese, who gave a measly five dollars with that thriving cheese store of hers. Some people.

"I can't imagine you'd change your opinion of people because of a list, G.T."

"I don't want to take the chance. We're running for everyone. Whoever gives, I'm grateful. Whoever doesn't, has a right. I'll talk to Adam."

G.T. pulled his truck into the parking lot of the Wisconsin Cheese Company, parked by a big trash compactor, said, "I'll be with you in a minute," and bowed his head.

I waited.

A few minutes passed and his head was still bowed. I figured he was praying. I checked my watch. We were already fifteen minutes late.

I wasn't sure what to do.

I coughed to remind him I was present.

Cleared my throat.

Yawned pretty loud.

Finally, he opened the truck's door and headed toward the factory.

"My name's G. T. Stoop, folks, and I'm running for mayor."

The midnight shift was just getting off. G.T. was standing in the cafeteria shaking as many hands as he could get to. Men and women in white coats and white hard hats were pressing in to see him the way you'd look at a curiosity. Weird cheese posters lined the walls.

CAN'T MISS SWISS

FETA? YOU BETA

PARMESAN POWER

I was doing my best to hand out the Students for Stoop newsletter and smile with flashing intensity. This was politics up close and personal.

Down the line he went asking people how they felt about things.

When a man said he didn't think politics could help anyone anymore, G.T. said one person can make a difference, two can lift a burden, and more than that can start a revolution.

When a woman said she hadn't voted for years, G.T. asked her why.

"There hasn't been anyone I trusted."

"I know what you mean," G.T. told her. "Trust doesn't always come right away in life, it has to be earned." He asked if she'd come to listen when he spoke; talk to people who know him. "If I can earn your trust in the next few months, will you vote for me?"

She was surprised at first, but met his gaze. "Yes, I will."

A man said, "I vote because I have to, not because I want to."

"I've felt that way in plenty of elections, too," G.T. admitted.

"Once I didn't vote. I learned I always felt better voting even if I wasn't happy with the choices."

Person after person. He dealt with each one like he or she was the only one in the room. This audience, I can tell you, was moved. Faces pressed in around him, open and smiling. People who looked like they'd just had a good meal.

I walked behind him passing out newsletters.

"Thank you for coming out to see G.T. today," I said over and over. "I hope you'll give this a read. We really need your support."

A short woman muscled through the crowd, stuck her hand out at G.T. "I'm voting for you, Stoop. Go out there and kick Millstone's butt."

G.T. shook her hand, laughing. "I appreciate it."

Then a few men in the back started shouting, "Kick Millstone's butt! Kick Millstone's butt!" And soon most of the crowd was hollering it.

Kick Millstone's butt!

Kick Millstone's butt!

The cheers swept us into the parking lot.

"Kicking butt wasn't the rallying cry I was going for," G.T. said as he drove to the commuter train terminal. "I'm non-violent."

"I think they know you'll fight for them, G.T. Those cheese people need a warrior."

"Hope, why do you think people need a warrior?"

We got to the train terminal late and missed the 8:53. There was no one on the platform.

"I'm not sure, really ... I think people are looking for someone who's strong to fight for them."

"But I'm not strong."

"You are in what you believe."

"But not in my body."

"Well ..." I wanted to change the subject.

"We have this need, Hope, for leaders to look good, sound good, and be perfectly healthy. But life's never been more clear to me than when I got this cancer."

I looked at his face, so determined, so tired. He was fighting for strength—pushing, straining to make this day count.

I slapped away the fear I had for his health and tried to enter into the courage.

What else can you do when you're spending the whole day with one of the finest men on this planet?

We survived the irritated kindergarten parents.

Managed to down the rubbery chicken in lukewarm white gravy at the Small Businessman's luncheon.

Headed off to the Tick Tock Clock Shop.

"What's your mother like, Hope?"

I sure wasn't expecting that question.

I squirmed. "You know Addie's not my mother."

"She told me that."

What else had she told him?

"My mother's a waitress, G.T."

I let that hang there between us, but it didn't quite tell the story.

"She's a much better waitress than she is a parent. She doesn't know how to be a mom, I don't think."

G.T. stopped at a light. "That's a lot for you to deal with."

"I've gotten pretty good at it."

Driving again.

"Your mother's missing out not knowing you as a daughter."

I'd never once thought of that.

I don't know why, but I almost started crying.

"You know what I've found out about disappointments?" G.T. asked.

I sniffed. "No."

"I think that if we face them down, they can become our strengths."

"Is that what you're doing with your cancer?"

"I'm trying, Hope. I'm sure trying."

Drinking weak coffee at the Tick Tock Clock Shop.

Six cancer survivors present, invited there by the owner, Beth Wisocki, who had breast cancer four years ago. This was her support group.

No handshaking here. Survivors hug.

"I've been clear of cancer for seven years," said a woman. "Faced death, bought my cemetery plot. They're going to have to wait awhile to bury me."

"Tell people," said a tall, thin woman with fiery eyes, "that life's being lived powerfully by many people with cancer. You tell this town that there's all kinds of things that make us sick. Disease is just one of them." She handed him a little card with flowers on it that read LIVE THE DAY, NOT THE CANCER.

As if on cue, every bell, gong, and cuckoo went off in the shop. It was three o'clock.

"This is my favorite time of day," Beth Wisocki shouted.

"Well, I sure know where to come if I'm ever feeling discouraged," G.T. shouted over the dings and dongs.

But he was doing too much.

I could see it on his face—it was drawn; gray; and stayed like that all the way to BVMRCC.

The intensity in this church basement.

Women had ten bingo cards going at once.

"We get a roomful of committed people like this behind us," G.T. whispered to me, "we could change the world."

An old woman said to him, "You don't look well enough to make it home, much less be mayor."

That cut deep.

"Do I look that bad?" he asked me.

I gave him the short-order truth. "You look like a plate of cold fried eggs. No offense."

"Lost my appeal, huh?"

"It's best the customers don't see the food in that condition."

"You don't mince words."

"Just garlic," I reminded him and led him to the truck.

13

We pulled into the Welcome Stairways at 8:45 P.M.

G.T. said he thought he'd stop in the kitchen and see how things were going and I said, while still being respectful, that from what I could see he needed to take care of himself and that did not include a stop in the kitchen. You'd think a man running for elected office would have the sense to listen to his body.

"All right. All right." He climbed the stairs slowly up to his apartment. "Thank you for coming with me today, Hope. You're a fine companion."

"I loved every minute of it, G.T."

I heard him unlock his door; shut it.

I went into the kitchen, planning to ask Braverman to make me a pork-chop sandwich. He tenderized the chop better than Addie did, and believe me, I would take that fact to my grave. He was working nights all this week.

I saw Addie at the grill instead, putting up orders.

"Where you been?" she asked, keeping her eyes on the food. Good cooks have eyes in the back of their heads like vampires.

I started telling her all the places G.T. and I had gone to, but she cut me off.

"We've got a situation here, Hope."

She was working in choppy, harsh movements. Addie only cooks like that when something's wrong.

"What . . . ?"

"It's Braverman." She took a deep breath. "He got beat up."

"What?"

"He's going to be okay. They broke a couple of ribs. He got some stitches over his eye. When he didn't show up for work, I just kept cooking."

I felt a chill in my spine.

Addie flipped three burgers, piled garlic mashed potatoes on a plate with balsamic chicken. "It's Brenda Babcock's day off. Flo said she took her mother into Milwaukee for hospital tests." Addie slammed a sauté pan. "What do you think of that coincidence?"

I closed my eyes.

My breath came out like it had been trapped.

I called Braverman's house, but his mother said he was sleeping. I called Jillian because I needed to talk to someone. I started crying over the phone and kept saying I didn't know what was wrong with me. I'm *not* a crier.

"You care for him," she said.

I bristled. "We *all* do."

"But I think, Hope, you care for him in a deeper way."

That's not what I needed to hear, even if it was, just possibly, true.

Batten down the hatches. That's what Brenda Babcock had said. I felt a huge wind picking up everything that wasn't nailed down.

8:35 A.M.

The wind beat strong.

G.T. was just leaving Braverman's house when I got there—worry and anger carved in his face.

I was holding the cactus I'd gotten for Braverman—$3.95 at Glugg's Grocery. Flowers didn't seem right; a cactus was manly.

I felt stupid holding it.

"He looks pretty bad, but you'll cheer him up." G.T. patted my shoulder. "I'm going to do everything I know to do to stop this madness." He marched down the walk, but he didn't seem strong.

The house next to Braverman's looked abandoned. A broken-down car without rear tires was across the street.

I rang the bell.

Braverman's mother answered, let me in. She was tall and looked scared. She walked with a cane.

"I'm Hope from the—"

"Oh, yes," she said, smiling. "He's talked about you."

He has?

I saw his twin sisters, Heidi and Heather.

"Are you his girlfriend now?" Heidi asked, giggling.

"No." I felt my face get hot. I put the cactus behind my back. "We work together. That's all."

Heather skipped off, shouting, "Eddie, your girlfriend's here."

Eddie?

I smiled dumbly at his mother.

"Eddie, your girlfriend's here!"

I've always appreciated being an only child.

A door down the hall creaked open. In the shadows I saw Braverman.

His face was swollen, he had a large bandage over his left eye. He stepped out into the light.

My heart broke for him. "Oh, Braverman . . ." I held out the cactus. "How do you feel?"

"Like three guys beat me up."

I walked over to him.

"There were three?"

He nodded.

"It must hurt a lot."

"I don't recommend the experience."

I almost took his hand, but didn't. We walked down the hall. All the furniture seemed old, not much on the walls. I didn't picture him living in a place like this. The nicest thing I could see was a big wooden case filled with books. The small, cramped kitchen had dirty dishes in the sink, a milk carton on the counter, cereal boxes lined side by side. He motioned me out onto the porch. It had two plastic chairs. I sat on one. He stood before me stiffly like Frankenstein.

I looked down at a little garden. The morning sun shone bright. It seemed to dance across the yard, touching the flowers.

No matter what happens, girl, remember the power of the light.

"Do you know who beat you up?" I asked.

"They didn't introduce themselves. They said I had a big mouth about the campaign and I'd better shut it." He looked at his feet. "I don't know which was worse—getting hit or not being able to hit back."

I swallowed hard.

"I was really worried about you, Braverman."

"Thanks."

A weird silence.

"For the first time in my life, Hope, I think I could have killed somebody. If I'd have broken free and gotten one of those guys I don't think I could have stopped hitting him."

"I think you would have stopped." I hoped he would have.

He clenched his hands. "I'm scared at how angry I feel. I'm yelling at my mom and my little sisters. I keep seeing those guys in ski masks holding my arms and I couldn't break free!"

I wasn't sure what to say. A big part of me wanted to hug him. "I know all about anger, Braverman." I told him about my boxing.

He was quiet.

"And sometimes," I added, "I have to remind myself who I'm mad at so I won't take it out on the wrong people."

"Like the cook," he offered.

We laughed.

He looked down again. "Will you do me a favor?"

"Sure."

He stood up straight, closed his eyes at the effort that took.

"Millstone's speaking at the Methodist church picnic on Saturday. I need you to help me get there."

He had to be kidding.

"I just need a ride. I'm not supposed to drive until the bandage comes off my eye. I don't think my mother will . . . you know . . ."

"Braverman, did they give you strong painkillers, or is your brain just naturally impaired?"

He thought about that.

"Both," he said.

A rash of teenagers signed up to work on G.T.'s campaign as news of Braverman's beating hit the streets and Jillian spread the word on-line.

G.T. stood on the steps in front of Town Hall. "I will not allow this evil to prosper! I demand a full investigation by Deputy Babcock to bring those criminals to justice!"

Sheriff Greebs strolled out the front door. "I'll be handling any investigations around here."

"I do not believe, Sheriff, that will lead us to the truth."

"That's your problem," snarled Greebs as he walked to his squad car.

On Thursday the *Mulhoney Messenger* carried this on the front page:

A POLITICAL LESSON
by E. A. Braverman

This week three men dragged me into an alley and beat me up. They took turns holding me down. They took turns hitting me. I didn't owe them money. I hadn't done anything to hurt them. They didn't take my wallet. All they tried to take was my right to support G. T. Stoop's candidacy. They told me I'd better shut my mouth about politics in this town.

I don't know their names or where they live, but I would like to say something to all three of them.

It didn't work.

Oh sure, you broke three of my ribs. I have stitches in my forehead and I won't be able to work for a while. But you've only made me more determined to speak out and find the truth about the corruption that has a hold of this town.

For a few days after the beating, I told myself that if I'd been stronger, I could have pushed you away. The truth is, you are the weak ones. And you've made your cause that much weaker by showing how low you would sink to get Eli Millstone reelected.

I hope the sheriff's office catches you, but even more than that, I hope that people will see the fear that's really behind your actions. You're afraid of the truth.

You know what?

You should be.

Saturday morning. The teenagers of Mulhoney had had enough.

I got Braverman his ride to the Methodist church picnic. Fifty-seven kids decided to join us.

My heart was thumping with anger and deep caring as Braverman dragged his bruised self into the big tent set up on the front lawn and stood smack in front of Eli Millstone, who was droning on about truth, justice, and the American way.

"Mr. Mayor! Could you explain what the sheriff's department is doing to find the three men who attacked me?"

Millstone was shocked at first, but looked at Braverman with fake compassion. "We're going to get to the bottom of what happened to you, son. I give you my word."

"Your *word?*" Braverman hobbled closer. "Mr. Mayor, your *word* isn't worth anything."

Adam raised his fist in the air and started the cheer.

"Tell the truth! Tell the truth!"

We screamed it loud until the tent poles shook.

Until finally Eli Millstone stormed out, fuming.

You think all teenagers care about are musicians and movie stars?

Spend some time in Wisconsin.

We'll blow your socks off.

On the mouse front, we had big news. The *Mulhoney Messenger* carried it on the front page. The paper was down to eight pages now; it used to be twenty, but Cecelia Culpepper vowed to keep publishing it no matter what.

The lab report showed no rodent hairs in the Welcome Stairways kitchen. The mouse had been dead for at least a week. It couldn't have come from our diner. That sweet couple had been arrested twice for passing bad checks.

"And the corker," said Deputy Babcock, sipping coffee at the counter, "is that couple said a man in Milwaukee paid them to do their mouse act in the Welcome Stairways."

"What kind of a person would do that?" Flo asked.

"I don't know," Brenda Babcock replied. "But I'm going to find out."

Days passed. Hot, muggy ones. Not that I've ever expected much else from July.

Braverman was in direct contact with his inner porcupine. He'd become consumed with "getting" Millstone.

Revenge of the Giant Grill Man.

He'd become a symbol of public outrage, walking around town with his bandage over his eye and his black-and-blue face. But, as Sid Vole said, it sure was a good reminder to the voters. "STOOP FOR MAYOR" was showing up on more and more lawns and bumper stickers, but the juggling, joking Braverman was gone. He was serious and fuming, morning till night.

I mentioned it to him gently after a campaign meeting.

"I swear to God," he vowed. "I'm not going to let Millstone win."

"I just don't think you should carry the whole campaign on your shoulders."

"Just lay off, Hope."

It really hurt me when he said that.

Braverman's injury was wreaking havoc in the kitchen. He couldn't work a whole shift. Addie was pulling killer hours. She tends not to suffer in silence. Once, G.T. rolled up his sleeves to help her, and in twenty minutes of them working side by side my whole future in Wisconsin could have gone up in smoke. Thankfully, G.T. saw it, too. He backed out gracefully and said, "Well, Addie, I sure don't want to ruffle your feathers any more than I have."

Addie muttered that if she had any feathers left it was only by the grace of God.

Out at the counter G.T. said to me, "You got any advice on how to get along better with your aunt?"

I looked at his determined face; felt he could take it. "G.T., truth is costly. You've got to give her full reign in the kitchen. There's no other way."

"Hands off, huh?"

"Completely."

G.T. looked at his hands and put them in his pockets.

G.T.'s energy was up and down. His fever had risen slightly, and his doctor said he had to avoid most people until his white blood count went higher. That scared all of us. G.T. said this would be part of his life for a while, but he was like a caged bull waiting to get free.

I was standing in his apartment, which was across the hall from ours. I'd brought up some of Addie's disease-fighting chicken soup with egg noodles. I'd triple-washed my hands with antibacterial soap and sprayed Lysol disinfectant on my sneakers.

I could tell he was hurting.

"How's Braverman?" he asked.

I kept it light. "He's healing. He's working things out."

A huge sigh. "How's it going downstairs?"

"Good. We're staying busy."

He slapped the table, stared at the oil painting on the wall of a little sailboat riding the waves of a choppy ocean, its sail puffed full with the wind.

"That's where I want to be," he said with irritation.

"You're a sailor?"

"Not much of one. I want to be out in the thick of it, Hope, not stuck in here like some *patient*."

I looked at the painting. "I feel like that boat sometimes."

"How so?"

"Well, sometimes I feel pretty small and the waves around me are big, but I still have this feeling that I'm going to make it to shore."

Harrison would have loved that.

G.T. smiled. "My mother painted it."

"She's good."

"She said it was how she saw troubles. A good sailor knows how to steer into the wind, to use the power to his advantage. You don't become a real sailor until you sail in a storm. Then you test what you know, you see what you and the boat and the wind are made of."

I looked at that painting for the longest time.

Thought of the high waves of my mom leaving me.

The big winds of Gleason Beal that almost capsized me.

"I wish there was another way to learn, G.T."

He flopped on the couch. "I don't like the process either." He picked up a beautiful piece of dark wood that was sitting on the coffee table; held it out to me. "Feel that."

It was smooth like glass.

"That piece of mahogany came from a ship that sailed the seas over a hundred years ago. See how deep the color is? It didn't start out that way. It was the pounding of the waves and the stretching of that vessel by the sea over the years that helped make this wood so beautiful."

I held the wood. Didn't want to put it down.

"I know how hard it is sometimes to be strong, G.T."

He looked at me with such kindness. "I know you do."

I covered the soup to keep it warm and hoped with all my heart that he'd get well.

Losing G.T. seemed like the worst thing that could ever happen.

We lost Sid Vole instead.

He'd been called to Virginia to provide mouth-to-mouth resuscitation to the campaign of a congressman who had visited a school and announced that Abraham Lincoln was the thirteenth president of the United States instead of the sixteenth. A little kid had corrected him and then the whole class started laughing. A TV camera had been there to capture the drama. The press was crucifying that man.

It was, Adam said, the ultimate test of the ultimate spin doctor.

But it meant we were down a consultant in G.T.'s campaign.

Not to mention an adult.

I was trying to write this all in a letter to Harrison and Miriam. Trying to explain my life up here with G.T.'s campaign and how important it was. Trying to explain why Braverman got beat up and the depth of our non-relationship.

There's this guy that I told you about before—I'm kind of interested in him, except we work together and we're really just friends. Sometimes I think he likes me and other times I don't think he does and I'm finding the whole thing really irritating.

Miffed in Mulhoney.

I walked over to my Replogle globe, which was sitting on my dresser. I gave it a slow spin, stopped it at Wisconsin.

Put my finger on Milwaukee. Moved it slightly to the left.

Mulhoney, of course, was not on the globe.

Such a small, hidden place in the world.

"I'm here, Dad." I said it louder than I'd expected.

I waited, listening.

Life has too many unsolved mysteries.

Some things become a mission, and Mr. Woldenburg became that for me. Every Friday he'd plunk down at the counter and order the same thing—grilled American cheese on white. I tried not to shudder.

Tried to introduce him to new food experiences, like grilled Swiss on seven-grain bread with sliced tomatoes.

"Had a grilled American on white every Friday for as long as I can remember." Hands on hips. Mr. Impatience.

I tried to get him to talk about anything.

He grunted instead.

I always tried to put in a few good words for G.T.'s candidacy, but he never responded. Once when people at the counter were talking about the election he announced, "I don't vote. Never have."

Never?

"I don't vote, the wife don't vote either. All politicians do is mess up the world."

Adam was sliding in for the kill, holding a Students for

Stoop newsletter, smiling like the Cheshire Cat. But Mr. Woldenburg waved him off. "Not going to read any propaganda."

He ate his sandwich and left a fifteen percent tip (fifty-seven cents).

You should vote, Mr. Woldenburg.

It might expand your world.

G.T.'s fever was down, but boy, was he dragging.

A few reporters got wind of G.T.'s campaign and came to town to interview him. A human interest story, they called it. Sid Vole had called a few newspaper editors that he knew. It was his parting gift to G.T.'s campaign—more publicity.

Braverman watched and listened like a sponge.

"What has the cancer taught you?" a reporter asked G.T.

"It's never too late to do the right thing," G.T. answered.

"Great," Braverman said, and wrote down the exchange on his pad.

There were MOS interviews (man on the street).

TOS interviews (teen on the street).

Some people, like Addie, refused interviews. I never did. I had a secret hope down deep that with all this media exposure, my father would somehow recognize my face, my name, *something*, jump into his Jaguar sedan and drive fast, but not recklessly, through the night to find me.

I was in the back office taking my break and feeding Anastasia. She'd been here for over a month and not much had changed. Her little mouth would start sucking, then she'd let the bottle drop. I'd put it back in her mouth; she'd try again. She sure was small and skinny.

"Okay," I told her, "you're real lucky I'm here because I had the same problem eating as you did when I was a baby. Sucking for food isn't a concept every baby gets right off and you've got to just deal with the stress because people are going to put their stopwatches to you and expect you to be doing things you're not ready for." I put the bottle near her mouth. She took a few more sucks, and couldn't hold on.

"Now the best thing you've got going for you is that your mother really cares about you. I know this is true because she's making the rest of us half nuts with all her worrying. My mother couldn't have cared less, and I bet that affected my eating in the beginning, so you're way ahead of the game in that department, Anastasia. I think you should feel pretty good about that."

I rubbed the bottle's nipple over her lower lip. I'd seen a veterinarian do that once at Miriam Lahey's house to get her dog to eat. Anastasia opened her mouth a bit.

"Suck," I said.

She did a little. "Not bad. I'm telling you, you get this eating stuff down, lots of things are going to fall into place. At some point, you might want to talk to your mom about your name because Anastasia is almost as big a challenge as the first one I got slapped with. But first things first. Eat, baby. You need the energy. Come on."

The bottle slipped out again.

I put my finger in her mouth to see what would happen. She grabbed on, started sucking.

"That's the stuff. I'm going to make the transfer now."

I moved my finger out of her mouth, brought the bottle in. Not much better.

"It's okay. We're just going to practice it. Do you know your mother loves you so much she lugged a collapsible crib to the diner so you could be here while she worked?" Anastasia was watching me now, smiling a little. "Another thing about your mom—do you know she can carry four captain's platters on her arm and not drop an orange slice? You've got an excellent person fighting for you. That's about the best thing a kid can have in life—somebody out there fighting for them. Try this bottle again." She didn't hesitate this time, took the bottle, drank longer than I've ever seen her.

She kept drinking, looking at me. I took a chance, put her little hands around the bottle, pressed them firm so she'd get the idea.

"Come on, Anastasia. Hold on." All of a sudden there was nothing more important to me than this baby holding this bottle herself.

There was a sniff behind me. I looked up to see Lou Ellen standing in the door, tears streaming down her face.

I wasn't sure what to say.

"You're a good mother, Lou Ellen."

She shook her head.

"You are. Believe me, I know the difference."

I took my hand off the bottle and for a few magic seconds

Anastasia was feeding herself. Lou Ellen was standing there by the door grinning through tears.

I was smiling at Anastasia and trying not to cry myself.

The thought kept hitting me over and over.

I wonder if my mother ever cried for me.

I walked slowly up the back stairs and crashed in the apartment, exhausted from everything. I never take naps, but I was going to take one today. I headed for my room; my soft, clean bed. I kicked off my shoes, getting ready for the experience.

"Brace yourself," Addie said to me from our kitchen.

"What?"

She appeared in the hall, stone-faced. Bad sign.

"No way to tell you except straight-out, Hope. Your mother's coming to visit."

"What?"

"She read about what's happening in town and she's coming up from St. Louis."

I felt this heavy cloud fall in the room.

Could see Deena filing her nails, telling me she loved me.

"I don't really want to see her now, Addie."

"She doesn't tend to ask permission. You know that."

"You know how weird those visits are."

"She's driving up, honey. She'll be here in a few days."

I flopped down in despair, chilled to the bone in the middle of summer.

It was my father who was supposed to be coming, not *her*.

*　*　*

I slammed plates the next day at the diner. Braverman was back at work. It was good to see him until he called me "Sunshine," and then I told him to back off.

I'm doing all I can to avoid stress. Ask Flo to take the six-top of truckers telling dumb-blonde jokes.

Tell Lou Ellen I'll pay her to wait on the young mother at table ten with the five children all under the age of seven.

I've got one hour to go on my shift and I have not committed murder in any form. I'm squeezing my hands and releasing them to get rid of the tension. I want the gloves on bad. I really want to hit the big bag.

That's when this hotshot reporter swings into the diner like he's God's gift to journalism. Adam Pulver is covered in STOOP buttons on his way out the door. The guy stops Adam and tells him he wants to talk to "some average Americans working on this campaign." Adam points to me and says, "Hope is average."

Gee, thanks.

This reporter saunters up and asks me how I, an average all-American teenager, feel about the campaign. I try to look distinctive, tell him how G.T. wants to bring the town together by telling the truth and not playing favorites.

"G.T. isn't fake like so many politicians, he really wants to help people, he's not in it for the power or the glory."

"Where is he now?" the reporter demands.

I know he's upstairs taking a nap because he's not feeling too well, but I don't think that's the right thing to say. Then I think that G.T. would probably want me to tell the truth, so I do.

"And *how*," the reporter asks, smirking, "do you expect a man who isn't feeling too well to run this town, or any town?"

My mind closes up.

The reporter asks me if I understand the question. I pour coffee into a man's cup instead of answering.

"*Why* would a teenager want to spend so much time on this campaign?"

I feel the heat on my face.

Point my number-two pencil at him.

"Because I never thought about what it means to be a citizen before working on this campaign. I just took it for granted. Now for the first time I see how I need to take a part in the process, I need to think about my place in society, I need to say no to corruption even though there's so much of it around. When you listen to G. T. Stoop, you understand the importance of being a honorable person, you get charged to fight for the truth, you get angry that so many politicians are playing games with people's trust."

"Are you old enough to vote?" he asks.

"No. None of us kids are."

Braverman's loud ahem from the kitchen.

"Except him."

I focus in on my order book like I'm figuring a check. I don't like this man. Don't trust him.

"What if he dies?" the reporter asks like he couldn't care less.

I don't want to think about that.

The reporter stands there waiting. He isn't going away.

I hold my order book tight. "Then everyone here, everyone

who's known him, will have seen that there are people who aren't trying to sell us down the river, aren't being dishonest behind closed doors. I don't know where you come from, mister. I don't know what kinds of people have let you down. But for me, *an average American teenager,* knowing there are real people in the public eye or anywhere who are trustworthy and kind makes the whole thing worth it."

The reporter writes down what I said.

"I hope you get it right," I tell him.

He smiles—not a mean one. Surprise.

"He's lucky to have you fighting for him. Can I use your name in the article?"

I tell him my name.

"Hope," he says, writing it down. "There seems to be a lot of that around here."

From the kitchen I hear the sound of clanging pots. "You've got that right!" Braverman shouts.

I was closing up the Welcome Stairways with Braverman, cleaning the ketchup and mustard bottles, filling the sugar bowls. Braverman put on his Brewers cap and asked if I was okay.

"My mother is coming to visit me."

"Is that good or bad?"

"Bad . . . some of each, maybe. I don't know."

Braverman sat at the counter, folded his big hands in front of him. His bandage was off his forehead. The long scar would take time to heal. "I've got a father like that."

"I'm sorry."

"I handle it. What else can you do?" He squeezed his hands when he said it.

"I guess I handle my mother, too. She's got some good qualities."

"I saw my dad just before you and Addie moved up here. He came into the diner, and I made him a pork-chop sandwich. He loved it; asked how it was made. We sat in a booth eating and talking about all kinds of things. I think meeting him here where I've really succeeded made a difference."

"I don't know where I'm going to see my mom."

"You should see her right here, Hope. Let her see you doing your job. You're the best waitress under thirty I've ever seen."

"Braverman, thank you."

I had to tell him. "She named me Tulip."

Braverman cocked his head. That didn't register.

"Tulip. Like the flower. It was my name for twelve years. I hated it. She'll probably call me that when she gets here."

Braverman looked like he was going to start laughing.

"I can't laugh about it yet, Braverman."

"Is it all right if I do?"

He didn't wait for permission. He lost it right there.

"*That's the worst name I ever heard in my life!* Tell her, Hope," he said between guffaws, "to never call you that again."

I looked down. He didn't know my mother, Deena the Mouth.

"*Tulip!*" he gasped. "*What was she thinking?*"

I started laughing now, too. I'd never laughed about the absurdity of it.

"I used to get nauseous in the spring when the tulips came up. There I was, walking through beautiful gardens, wanting to puke. Easter was torture."

Braverman was holding his side, laughing. He pulled himself together finally. "But you're over it."

I looked at him.

"You're not Tulip anymore, no matter what she says."

He was right.

He took off his cap and bowed. "I think Hope is the perfect name for you."

And with that he walked out the door.

My heart flipped at that one.

15

I saw my mother before she saw me.

Saw her walking up the welcome stairways, tossing her long, straight hair that was black like india ink. She was wearing tight jeans, heels, a beaded T-shirt, and sunglasses. She had a big canvas bag that read MIAMI MADNESS. Between her too-big earrings and the collection of bracelets on her left arm, she made quite a racket, which caused most people in the place to look at her as she made her way to the counter. She plopped on a counter stool, took off her sunglasses. Her eyes were heavily made up with the kind of mascara that "extends and magnifies." I stood off by the coffee urn feeling a primal pull to the woman who gave me life and no connection to her whatsoever.

From the kitchen, Addie raised a spatula—the cook's hello.

My mother waved excitedly.

My turn.

Remember, I told myself. The well is dry.

I grabbed a coffeepot so I'd have something to hold on to,

walked to the counter, and wasn't sure how to get her attention because she was reading the menu like some people read a good mystery novel. So what do you do when your own mother who you haven't seen for three and a half years is sitting there at your counter not even looking for you?

She'd come for lunch, I guess, not me.

"Hi, Mom."

Her head cocked at the unfamiliar word—*Mom*, not *hi*—her eyes got big and excited, she grabbed my hand with her too-long ruby nails. "Now don't tell me this is really you!"

Deena Does Motherhood.

"It's really me," I said, smiling weakly.

"Tulip, I can't tell you—"

I put my hand over hers. "My name is Hope now, Mom."

"Oh well, I know, but I'll just never get used to—"

"I need you to get used to it."

Deena didn't like that.

Her light-blue eyes lost their sparkle.

She took her hand away.

She smiled fake. "I'll *try.*"

You do that.

I'd read a book about anger once and how people can have it but deny they do, so it comes out in other ways. Passive-aggressive behavior, the book called it.

Now Deena was back to reading the menu like I wasn't there. I wanted to start screaming, *Why did you bother coming back? Why don't you just go for good?*

She ordered a grilled-chicken sandwich (semolina roll,

avocado, mango mayonnaise) with sweet potato chips and iced tea. She ordered it like I wasn't her daughter.

I walked to the galley, fighting tears. I had to pull myself together.

There's no crying allowed at lunchtime rush.

I called in her order to Braverman and Addie. As I said, "Mango mayo on the side," I almost keeled over in grief.

Addie leaned forward. "You want to take a break?"

I shook my head. I didn't want to be alone.

I just stood there holding on to a big refill jar of sweet pickle relish. Every time my mother moved, I could hear her clatter.

Braverman said, "You want to be a clown?"

"What?"

He took out a red sponge clown nose, put it over his nose, and raised one eyebrow.

He looked completely absurd.

I started giggling.

He took it off, handed it to me. "Wear it for a while."

"Now?"

"Yeah."

I held the red clown nose; stood there for the longest time with the flurry of lunchtime pounding all around me.

I put the nose over my nose and stared at Braverman, who started laughing.

Addie cracked up, too.

I turned around as Flo was coming round the corner. She stopped dead in her tracks, stared, and grinned.

My heart was breaking, but this nose had power.

I hit the counter, nose and all. And you should have seen those people's faces, including my mother's. Everyone was laughing and pointing and my mother started chuckling. I did a little twirl getting someone ice water—you can do things like that in a red clown nose.

I felt my gestures getting broader and kids were pointing and laughing and all of a sudden I heard the two dings from the galley—my signal. I went to pick up my mother's order with the mango mayo on the side. I stood in front of her, first flicking off the counter before her with a towel, like she was really important. I placed the dish dramatically in front of her and bowed.

"That's my daughter," she said to the man next to her. "Her name is . . ." She caught herself. "Hope."

"Good name," the man said.

Well, that got me flying.

I topped off coffee for the people at the counter, suggested dessert to a couple in the corner booth, blasted through some takeout orders, gave a teething baby an ice cube to suck on, which shut it right up. Mom was watching me and I was glad because I didn't drop anything, didn't spill, didn't get upset when Yuri cleared away plates before the people at table six had finished their lunch. And when I grabbed my heart and leaned into their booth begging for another chance, I'd bring them more food, they laughed and said sure, they weren't in a hurry.

Everyone was watching me and leaving big tips. A little boy said, "I didn't know there were *girl* clowns."

Stick around, kid, you might learn something.

I did a funny walk to the ice cream serving area, lifted a maraschino cherry from a dish, waddled back to his table, and plopped the cherry on *his* nose.

Little kids were coming up to touch the nose and I gave every one of them cherries. They were all walking around trying to hold the cherries on their noses. Sucking in the glory of being a clown.

That's when G.T. walked into the diner looking tired as anything, but he took one look at me and started laughing, too.

I bowed low to the crowd, who applauded. Then I took the nose off and gave it back to Braverman.

"You keep it," he said.

I stood there feeling the spongy red ball that had turned discouragement into hope.

I was sitting with my mother in the corner booth. Addie had sat with us for a while, but she had entrees to get ready for dinner. They sure had a funny relationship. I could tell Deena looked up to Addie—she was always searching Addie's face for a response to whatever she said. I could also tell that Addie would never, ever believe that.

It was almost time for Mom to leave. She had to drive back down to St. Louis to meet her new boyfriend, Eduardo. Mom liked men who had names ending in vowels.

"What happened to Dino?" I asked. He was the last one she had mentioned.

She flicked her fingernails on the table. "Old news."

Twice I'd felt like putting the clown nose on again.

The first was during the boxing exchange.

MOM: "Are you still boxing?"

ME: "I gave that up a long time ago."

MOM: "Thank God, I was so concerned that you were doing that, I can't tell you. You were such an angry child."

She always brought things back to the past. "I worked it through, Mom."

The second was during her fond farewell when she kept telling me how she hated having to go, it was wonderful to see me, and we'd have to do this again real soon.

The best part was when she gave me waitressing tips. I wrote them down on the back of my order book. I'd write them in the Best of Mom book later.

Keep cut lemon wedges under the counter so you don't have to go to the kitchen for them—saves time.

Keep a bottle of Tylenol in your pocket in case a customer has a headache. You get rid of that headache for them, you'll see it in your tip.

Don't just ask people what kind of dressing they want. Tell them what you've got—they might try something new and be grateful.

She gave me a quick, flimsy hug that people give when they're not sure about themselves or you. She hugged Addie the same way.

Then she said to me, "You're quite a waitress now." And she left in a cloud of too much perfume.

I wish like anything my mom would treat me as well as she treats her customers.

Ask me what I need.

Take the time to see how I'm really doing.

See that I'm hungry to know my real parents.

But that word *real*—it makes it seem like Addie hasn't done much, and that's a lie. She's done everything. I need to say my *biological* parents. But when you're in food service, you understand that sometimes you're making up for people in your customers' lives who haven't been too nice. A lonely old woman at the counter just lights up when I smile at her; a tired mother with a screaming baby squeezes my hand when I clean up the mess her other child spilled.

You know what I like most about waitressing? When I'm doing it, I'm not thinking that much about myself. I'm thinking about other people. I'm learning again and again what it takes to make a difference in people's lives.

I watched Deena sashay down the welcome stairways; I felt sad and free at the same time.

Welcome, friend, from whichever way you've come. May God richly bless your journey.

I pulled the clown nose from my pocket, stuck it on my face, and headed up the back stairs to the apartment.

16

August was upon us. Hot, sticky, just like New York.

I was in the kitchen, about to go on my break. Braverman was working the grill.

Addie and G.T. were there, too. They were getting along a whole lot better now that G.T. had stopped interfering in the kitchen. G.T. was eating a hunk of her meatloaf and a piece of her prize apple pie, which looked like excellent break food to me. I sliced some of each as he said, "Addie, this is the finest meatloaf in America."

Addie waited for the next part because people were always saying something even greater about her apple pie.

"This is my favorite thing of yours," he said, cutting another slice of meatloaf.

If this were a cartoon, steam would have come from Addie's ears.

"What about the pie?" she asked loudly.

"Oh, it's fine pie. I like your pie. But, Lord in heaven, woman, I *love* your meatloaf."

I was trying to gesture to G.T. to say something better about the pie.

"Most people feel the pie is the standout dish in my repertoire," she snarled.

"They haven't had the meatloaf."

Addie said, trust her, they'd had the meatloaf.

G.T. laughed. "Oh, there's plenty of apple pies in this old—" and thankfully he realized the error of his ways. "But your apple pie is the finest of them all."

Addie said it was nice of him to say so, but it wasn't either.

"Oh yes," G.T. declared. "It is the best."

Addie said, well, she appreciated the compliment, she'd had her share of apple pie compliments, certainly, but it wasn't anything special.

And that was when G.T. said kind of quiet, "Addie, I don't mean to put you on the spot, and you can say no if you want to, but would you like to have dinner with me?"

Braverman froze.

Flo stopped making coffee.

Addie looked right at him and said they had dinner just about every night.

"I mean," G.T. said, laughing, "in another restaurant."

Addie asked what was wrong with her cooking.

It had been a while since she'd been asked out. Longer than me even.

G.T. said there was a place in Redding a half-hour away that had terrific lamb shanks—not as good as hers, of course, but what about it?

"I've got three pies and hash browns that aren't done yet

and two roast chickens with wild-rice stuffing that still need heavy butter basting."

"After that, then."

Addie said all right. She'd meet him at eight o'clock in the parking lot and he said he'd be happy to come to her door—it was only across the hall.

"The parking lot or nothing," said Addie.

G.T. nodded and headed out the back door.

Addie walked into the walk-in cooler and shut the door.

I stood there not moving.

"It's about time," said Flo from the galley window. "Those two are made for each other."

I'd never once thought of that.

I caught up with Flo at the counter. "*How* are they made for each other?"

She laughed. "They love food. All they do is work. They both have strong personalities and they've learned how to enjoy each other's ways. Where have you been?"

"Took him long enough," Lou Ellen chimed in.

Not that anyone asked me, but I wasn't sure if this was a very good idea.

For starters, there was the cancer.

I went back in the supply closet to get mayonnaise because I needed to be somewhere to think.

I was looking through the sauces and the mustards wondering how all this started.

Maybe it was just a friendly gesture after all her hard work, but something told me it was more than that.

And Addie's face had gotten all pink like an out-of-season

strawberry and she'd looked, briefly, kind of feminine when he asked her.

Addie's had her share of heartache with men. A few years ago, when she found out that her no-good husband, Malcolm, who deserted her, had died, she cried her heart out, not from love, but from all that got wasted between them. She'd been thinking about getting a divorce, but didn't know where he was for thirteen years—she thought about getting him declared legally dead, which, she said, wasn't much of a reach if you'd watched him slumped in his Barcalounger in front of the TV watching football. Addie said she once stuck her compact mirror under his nose to see if he was still breathing.

I didn't want anyone to get hurt, and I didn't want anything to be more complicated than it was.

Braverman came into the supply closet looking for something. I knew he'd heard the whole thing.

"I don't want to talk about it, Braverman."

Braverman cleared his throat like he was choking.

I checked his face for signs of distress like they taught me to when I learned the Heimlich maneuver. I used it once at the Blue Box on an Iranian cabdriver who was choking on a chicken bone and probably would have died if I hadn't stepped in.

Braverman was breathing fine; just acting strange.

Finally he said, "Hope, do you want to have dinner with me sometime?"

I dropped a plastic bottle of Gulden's.

We looked at it on the floor. Neither of us picked it up.

"I mean, I know we have dinner a lot when we're working.

I meant out someplace. Together." Braverman picked up the Gulden's bottle, handed it to me. He coughed. "A date."

I said, "What is this, an epidemic?"

I backed out the door and left Braverman in the supply closet.

I don't get asked out too much either.

It was 1:00 A.M. when Addie swung in from her off-the-premises dinner with G.T.

Not that I was waiting up for her or anything.

I thought 1:00 A.M. was a little late for older people to be coming in.

"Was it all right?" I asked her.

"It was fine."

"What aspect of the definition of fine was it?"

"We had a decent time."

I've been to Walgreen's and had a decent time.

"Give me something here," I demanded. "A crumb."

"Does it bother you that we had dinner?"

"*Yes.*"

"Well, it bothers me, too. I'm going to bed."

And she did just that.

I was living in a world of mixed signals.

Braverman said everything was fine, but everything had changed.

He didn't even make eye contact with me at the diner. He muttered things that only applied to my orders.

Mayo on the side, right?

Medium rare on the burger?

G.T. and Addie were impossible to read.

Once I saw him hug her in the kitchen.

Twice I saw them have enormous fights over Addie's attempted change to the pork-chop sandwich—putting it on a semolina roll instead of the traditional hard roll. G.T. won both times. Some things, he said, could not be made better.

I sure needed to make something better.

10:30 P.M.

Braverman was cleaning the grill.

Flo filled the last saltshaker, waved good-bye, and headed home. I took the clown nose from my pocket, put it on, tiptoed into the kitchen, and said to Braverman's back, "I owe you an apology."

He stiffened slightly, turned around.

I gave him my toothpaste-ad smile.

Tension left his face. He started to laugh.

I grinned. "This really great guy I know gave me this nose to help me put things in perspective."

"It works," he said.

I took a breath.

"I need to tell you that I would love to go out with you, Braverman, but I'm scared to do it. That's why I acted like a jerk when you asked me."

"Because we work together."

"Yeah."

"I'm worried about that, too."

I took the nose off, trying to be more attractive. "How worried are you about it?"

He sighed. "It could be a problem."

I moved a step closer.

"You could start thinking that I'm always going to cook your orders first."

"And you could start thinking that I wouldn't bug you when things are backed up."

Braverman laughed. "I'd never think that."

We stood there grinning at each other.

Braverman looked out at the empty diner. "We could have a trial run. Are you hungry?"

"Yeah..."

"Pork-chop sandwiches for two?"

My heart did a back flip. "Perfect."

He got the chops from the refrigerator, put them through G.T.'s old tenderizer, sprinkled them with seasoned salt and pepper, turned up the grill. He didn't say anything, just moved with the rhythm of the short-order dance.

My heart was beating fast. I couldn't stop smiling. I got two salads, put Addie's special mustard vinaigrette over them, piled on extra tomatoes.

Braverman took two clean dishcloths from the shelf, went out on the floor, and put them over table two in a diamond pattern like they were a fancy tablecloth. He walked to the register, rang up the meal, put money in the cash drawer, took the little vase of flowers by the cash register and put it on our table. He came back to the kitchen, toasted two hard rolls, put them on plates with lettuce and orange slices, and assembled the sandwiches. He layered the two plates on his left arm, grabbed his candle—the one he used when he sliced onions—and brought everything to the table. He lit the candle and grinned at me.

I got two 7UPs and walked over.

We sat down.

Braverman raised his glass and clinked it with mine.

I might as well have been in a prom dress, I felt so special.

We talked and laughed until midnight right there in the Welcome Stairways. And when dinner was over he said, "Hope, would it be okay if I kissed you?"

"You mean now?"

"Well, yeah. Did you have something else to do?"

I stood up fast. "Not a thing."

It was an excellent kiss—the kind where you feel your stomach burn hot and you know it's not from indigestion. We stood there for a while, arms around each other, not saying anything.

Then we looked at the dirty dishes on our table. Jarred back to reality.

I sighed. "I'll wash."

He blew out the candle. "I'll dry."

We cleared the table and walked back to the kitchen.

This is the downside of food service.

17

"Must be something in the water around here," Flo said the next day when she saw Braverman and me holding hands in the supply closet.

Addie pulled me aside. "What's going on with you and Braverman?"

I told her.

Well, Addie said, she'd been expecting it.

"What's going on with you and G.T.?" I asked.

She was saved from answering by the sound of the kitchen timer. "My hazelnut pound cakes are ready," she announced and left me standing there.

"It's a fair question," I shouted after her.

School.
It came up on me like indigestion.
I wasn't ready to go back, not even to be a junior.
Unfamiliar halls.
Unfamiliar teachers.

I'd been feeling so at home in Mulhoney working at the diner and being involved in G.T.'s campaign. Now suddenly I felt new and odd again.

I was ahead in math and English and behind in science and history. I had to take sophomore ethics class as a *junior* even though I'd taken it in Brooklyn. Wisconsin ethics takes a year to go through. Brooklyn's Type A—you only need a semester.

I slogged through my first week and managed to find all my classes. My English teacher liked my writing. She said I had "creative boldness." My history teacher said I had yet to "grasp the value of stating a clear thesis." I've always been a person who meanders around to find truth. This is death in the five-paragraph essay.

In political science, my best class, Mr. Sage said, "We're living a political science lesson right now in Mulhoney. We're going to examine this local election and see how it speaks to us on a larger scale."

That sounded interesting, but I wanted to be back full-time at the diner working with Braverman instead of only part-time after school and on the weekends.

We were having the best time working together, too, except when he'd make a mistake on an order and I'd have to be an advocate for my customer. I always mentioned it sweetly.

"You didn't say hold the bacon, Hope."

"Braverman, I said it twice."

"You must have said it to someone else."

"I said it to *you*."

Clang.

"*Don't* clang pots at me."

Other than that, hope was in the air.

Addie introduced the Keep Hoping sandwich and instantly it became a comfort-food classic.

Anastasia started holding her bottle like a drowning person clutching a life preserver. Even when it was empty, she wouldn't let go.

Flo said it was what we all had to do to get G.T. elected. Hold on to what we know is right and not let anyone take it from us.

And then, on September 29, we got the news we'd all been waiting for.

G.T.'s doctors declared that he was in remission.

You have to understand the full light that was released in G.T.'s face when he came back from the hospital with Pastor Hall and gave us the news. It was the kind of light that could open a daylily in the middle of a long, cold night.

He walked into the kitchen, walked up to Addie and told her.

She started crying.

"Okay," he said. "I think we need to get married."

We all froze at that one.

Addie looked right at him. "You don't have enough to do these days? You need something else on the schedule?"

Everything I am I owe to this woman.

The news of G.T.'s remission swept through town like a whirlwind that couldn't be stopped.

Then we got more good news.

Brenda Babcock arrested the two thieves who'd burglarized Adam's house. They were found at a pawnbroker's shop in Madison trying to sell Mr. Pulver's campaign button collection. Both thieves had the same name, too.

Carbinger.

"She's closing in," Flo said to me. "And we've got ourselves one nervous sheriff."

Three days later we had a blur of misinformation.

The sheriff said he was releasing the Carbingers—there was no evidence linking them to the crime.

Brenda Babcock said the Carbingers had agreed to a plea bargain with the district attorney to tell what they knew. They knew a lot. They said they were paid by the Real Fresh Dairy to frighten people who opposed the mayor, like Braverman. They claimed the sheriff had been paid off, too, to turn his head while they robbed houses.

Sheriff Greebs denied everything.

Cranston Broom from the dairy said he was appalled, disgusted, and very, very innocent.

Mayor Millstone said it was all a trick by the opposition to hurt his campaign.

TELL THE TRUTH, blared the *Mulhoney Messenger*.

The polls showed G.T. pulling seven points ahead of Eli Millstone.

We got revved like the Gospel of Grace van that had just gotten a new carburetor for the occasion.

It's interesting how polls take over a campaign. My political science teacher, Mr. Sage, said it was part of our society's need to know the score before the game is over.

G.T. put on a full court press to convince Addie that they should get married ASAP.

"I've got six chickens to roast, pies that need to be baked."

He laughed. "Can't you put your to-do list down for anything?"

But now the rightness of them getting married seemed to be hitting me from everywhere. I'd been so afraid, deep down, that G.T. would get sicker. I'd been afraid to think about what it could mean for me personally if he married Addie.

He would be my father, sort of.

Everything in me wanted to start dancing around the room at that thought, but just as fast, another one hit: What if G.T.'s not thinking of it that way?

That would be all-out awful.

I was in my room leafing through The Dads.

I'd always thought my dad was going to have a trench coat and thick hair and be pretty young and healthy. But that's the problem with fantasy, when the thing you want shows up, you have to regroup visually because it's never the way you picture it. A skinny bald guy in remission would not have made it into this collection.

But G.T. was better than all these trench-coated fantasy fathers put together.

I held Edgar, my pelican, smoothed back my hair.

"Well, Dad, it's sure taken you long enough to find me, not

that I'm complaining, but now I'm expecting you to do the right thing." I said the last part pretty loud.

I waited.

And hope fluttered in the room like a butterfly getting ready to light.

Braverman and I were driving home from the Octoberfest held in the little park off Grimes Square. Octoberfest is a German celebration that gets a lot of play in Wisconsin. It has real pluses and minuses. Pluses: sausage, coarse-grain rye bread, and apple strudel. Minuses: two guys playing an accordion and a tuba.

Braverman touched the back of my neck in that way that made me shiver. He smiled at me, turned on the radio in his old Toyota, and we couldn't believe what we heard.

Why can't G. T. Stoop tell the truth about his health? An unidentified, high-ranking hospital administrator verified that Mr. Stoop's leukemia has gone into his brain. It's just a matter of time before we all see what the doctors already know.

Is your future worth that risk?

Vote for Eli Millstone if you care at all about the future of Mulhoney.

Braverman pulled over on the side of the road. We sat there stunned.

It was a lie as sure as anything.

And that lie played three times an hour on radio and TV until people were saturated with falsehood.

G.T. denied it.

His doctor denied it.

But it kept pressing the deception over and over.

My teacher Mr. Sage said if you hear a lie often enough, it begins to sound like the truth.

Why can't G. T. Stoop tell the truth about his health?

Why?

Why?

Why?

My head pounded with fury. I couldn't focus. Blew off my homework three days running.

Cecelia Culpepper screamed for fairness on the front page.

Braverman and I went knocking on doors to try to calm the storm and saw firsthand how frightened people were. Jillian went on-line to alert the teen troops.

We hit the phones and called voters.

Braverman put out a new issue of the Students for Stoop newsletter with the headline ANATOMY OF A LIE.

But it was like watching floodwaters rise. There didn't seem to be anything we could do about it.

Al B. Hall drew his church together to pray.

G.T. started losing points in the polls.

Sid Vole was calling from the road, saying the only thing to do was hit back hard. Blow for blow.

"No sir," G.T. said. "I don't play like that."

G.T. kept his grueling schedule, talking to people until he was ready to drop.

People with STOP STOOP posters followed him everywhere.

We were working as hard as we could to get the truth out. The hospital even denied the report, showed G.T.'s medical records.

But the lie was everywhere and it was winning.

He called upon everyone to read his doctor's report, but what you didn't read was how his brain has been affected by the cancer.

He called upon churches and civic groups to support him knowing full well that he only has a few more months to live.

G. T. Stoop wants to be our mayor so much, he will lie, cheat, and misrepresent himself and his condition to get a few moments of glory.

On Election Day, vote for truth and health.

Reelect Eli Millstone.

The polls had G.T. neck and neck with Millstone now. One poll showed him three points behind.

"You going to listen to a *poll?*" Al B. Hall shouted from his pulpit. "Or your *soul?*"

Election Day.

Close to the longest day of my life.

We were everywhere.

Making last-minute campaign phone calls, passing out newsletters and buttons, cheering on the Gospel of Grace Evangelical van that shuttled back and forth bringing G.T.'s supporters to the polls.

Shouting foul when big groups of Millstone supporters went through town tearing down G.T.'s posters.

Hoping with all we had that we'd done enough.

"We're going to make it," Braverman said, and kissed me on the forehead, and went off to vote.

I sensed the hope building.

We all did.

I'd never been part of something so important before.

When I left Brooklyn I would have paid money to get out of making this move. Now, here I was, working with other kids to help get a good man elected. Here I was with the greatest boyfriend of the twenty-first century.

The polls closed at 9:00 P.M.

It was going to be close.

But we could feel the victory in our hearts. We hung on to that faith and wouldn't let go.

Back to the Welcome Stairways to wait and eat and wait some more.

Addie served us light and fluffy Victory Waffles with butter and warmed maple syrup.

We told ourselves how G.T. was going to pull it off.

How sweet it was going to be and we weren't going to be bad winners.

At 11:23 the results finally came in.

G.T. had lost by 114 votes.

There were simply no words.

Only tears.

18

You don't understand the power of loss when it first hits you like a baseball coming fast from an out-of-control pitcher. You reel back stinging from the blow.

It's the third day after an injury when the pain really starts to throb.

I'd known enough blows in my life, but this one had a special sting.

When a good man gets beaten by a bad one it makes you not want to get up in the morning.

It makes you hate the whole world.

"Well, we sure gave it all we had," G.T. said. "We made an inroad in people's consciences."

But I didn't think we'd made enough of one, or we'd have won.

I wasn't accepting Miss Congeniality for anything.

Lots of people were having this problem.

Adam was bitter about everything. "Millstone stole this election! We should have fought dirt with dirt!"

Sid Vole, whose candidate in Virginia had won, had personally called the governor of Wisconsin to see what could be done about it. After two weeks of intense checking, the official word was out: There were no signs of election tampering.

The results stood.

G.T. seemed a little lighter without the burden of campaigning on his shoulders. Addie said she had never much wanted him to be mayor anyway.

"Losing," G.T. offered, "isn't anything to be ashamed of." He told every campaign worker personally how much he appreciated how we'd worked for him. When he came to me he said, "Hope, I want you to know how much your strength supported me these many months. You've got an inner courage that is a powerful thing to witness. I thank you for bringing that up here. I really needed it."

I didn't know what to say.

Pastor Hall said this was one of those times when we just had to trust the Lord's ways.

I wasn't trusting anything.

The few reporters left in town had done what they called "postmortems" and moved out because we weren't important anymore.

I tried to pull from the power in my name, but everything hopeful in me was dead.

We limped through November, having a depressing Thanksgiving even though the food was brilliant.

"You can't enter a political campaign without accepting the fact that you might lose," Mr. Sage told our class.

He had gotten a copy of the voting statistics from the

election, which showed us who voted and who didn't, not who they voted for. Eighty-five percent of the adult population in Mulhoney voted. "I want you to be proud of these numbers. You were responsible for the highest voter turnout this town or any town has ever seen.

"I want you to think about all the people who registered to vote that probably wouldn't have if you hadn't been involved. I want you to try to recognize how you all learned to have a voice in the system."

And you could have knocked me over with a cheap tip when I saw the name of my cranky customer, Mr. Woldenburg, there on the voting roster. He and his wife. They'd voted! They'd taken part in the process.

We had to write a paper on what we remembered most about the campaign, what we thought our biggest contribution was. I wrote about passing out brochures and campaigning with G.T. I wrote about Mr. Woldenburg and how you never really know sometimes when you're making a breakthrough with certain people.

Mr. Sage wrote in the margin of my paper, "One person touching many."

"What kind of a world is this when Gleason Beal gets away clean and free and G. T. Stoop gets beaten by a crook?" I asked Braverman.

He hugged me hard. "I'm the wrong one to ask, Hope."

We spent lots of time hugging. At least something felt good.

I was in the A & P, looking for boxes of macaroni and cheese that I hid under my bed and made on the sneak when

Addie wasn't home. Addie *never* cooked from mixes. That's when I saw Mr. Woldenburg, my best success of the whole election. He hadn't been in the diner for a few weeks. I looked in his shopping cart. He had two packages of cheddar cheese, no American. Will wonders never cease?

"Hi, Mr. Woldenburg. Remember me?"

His eyes squinted. "You harped on me to vote more than a human has the right to."

I laughed. "I'm sorry it seemed that way, but I'm glad you and your wife voted, Mr. Woldenburg. That's terrific!"

"What in the world are you talking about, girl?"

"You voted, Mr. Woldenburg. I don't know if you voted for Eli Millstone or G. T. Stoop, but you took part in the election process, and that's a really good thing."

He looked at me like I'd lost my mind.

"I wasn't checking up on you, sir. I was just looking at the voting records and your name was there along with your wife's. It made my day, I'll tell you, when I saw you'd done it."

"That's the biggest fake I ever heard. I didn't register. I didn't vote. And neither did the missus."

I looked at his stern face.

"Mr. Woldenburg—you're not just kidding me?"

"I work two jobs. I don't have time for kidding or voting."

I tried to process this.

"Mr. Woldenburg, your and your wife's names were on the official election list as having registered and voted."

"Don't care if you saw it written in the sky. *We didn't do it.*"

My heart was in my larynx. "Will you tell what you just told me to the Election Board?"

He said he wasn't going out of his way.

"They'll come to you!" I didn't know if they would, but I was willing to drag them.

The Election Board sent workers out to get the truth— covering Mulhoney like cockroaches in a cheap fourth-floor walk-up, checking every registered voter's vote against whether they actually voted or not.

Braverman was doing big-time spatula tricks in the kitchen again.

At the end of ten days, we had a new ball game.

One hundred and twenty registered voters on the official books claimed they never registered, much less voted.

Eli Millstone was political toast.

A few reporters proclaimed us a hot spot again.

Then Braverman and Adam led the students of Mulhoney High to circle Town Hall with banners and posters, shouting down dishonesty in government. It was the third week in December, and Wisconsin was a vast, frozen tundra. My screaming taunts turned to ice crystals the minute they left my mouth. I mentioned to Adam that it would be warmer protesting *inside* Town Hall, but he said we needed to be poised against the pureness of the freshly fallen snow to make the point that we, the teenagers of Mulhoney, were not going to take this anymore.

We stood firm, 297 frozen teenagers dressed like Eskimos it was so mind-numbingly cold, and held a candlelight vigil outside Town Hall singing "We Shall Overcome." And as our united voices rose in force, Adam Pulver marched through the crowd, stood at the door of Town Hall, and shouted, "Mr. Mayor, we, the teenagers of Mulhoney, demand to live in a town that is not governed by lies and deceit. *We demand your resignation!*"

Adam raised his hands, embracing the spirit of the season, and started shouting, "Time to go! Ho, ho, ho!"

We shouted it into the night until we thought our voices would give out, but they didn't—we were too strong and too fed up.

You don't understand the power you have until you use it, that's what my boxing coach used to tell me.

Finally, Eli Millstone's spokesperson came out as dawn broke against the sky. She read a statement from the mayor.

"I have served this town faithfully as mayor, but it appears now that I cannot finish my third term because of the dissension of certain factions. I am resigning. I pray that Mulhoney will continue on in the great tradition I have set."

"We might change it a little bit!" Braverman shouted.

The whoop that went up from all of us was great and full. Al B. Hall showed up with seven GOG members, and they began serving us hot chocolate and doughnuts from the Gospel van. We stayed there shivering and savoring the victory.

Pastor Hall said we had shouted down the walls of Town Hall just like Joshua shouted down the walls of Jericho.

It happened finally on January 12 at high noon.

G. T. Stoop stood on the platform that Eli Millstone had

built for himself, put his hand on the Bible, and took the oath of office. He swore to uphold the laws of Mulhoney to the best of his ability, so help him God. Everyone there knew we'd heard an honest man make a pledge that he would take to heart every day he was mayor.

Al B. Hall stood before us, his wool coat blowing open in the winter wind, and offered the prayer.

"Lord God Almighty, bless your servant, Gabriel Thomas Stoop, with the fullness of your wisdom, strength, and courage. Give him a fierce faith to lead this town and let the love and kindness you've placed inside him pour out toward all."

Snow started falling like a promise, dusting the streets with anticipation of good things to come.

Everyone there felt the hope.

Addie said it was like the thrill she got shoving a raw plucked chicken into the oven and knowing that in a little while she'd have a soul-satisfying entree.

It takes a great cook to pull life truth from poultry.

19

The first thing G.T. did as mayor was appoint Brenda Babcock as sheriff. Ex-Sheriff Greebs was up to his earlobes in corruption charges courtesy of the state's attorney. The second thing G.T. did was to slap a fat fine on the Real Fresh Dairy and give them sixty days to pay their back taxes or the town would take them to court.

The third thing he did was marry Addie.

It was a simple ceremony with breathtaking food.

Addie cooked everything, even though people said she shouldn't. It was her day to shine. I was the only person who understood fully that Addie only half shone if she wasn't cooking.

She was a bear to live with during the last week because she'd put together a four-course dinner for over one hundred people and she hadn't gotten her wedding dress yet. I tried mentioning this to her and didn't get far.

"The bordelaise sauce is in the toilet, Hope, because I can't get decent mushrooms. You want me to think about fashion when my sauce is at risk?"

I went out, found her a dress, and dragged Braverman with me.

I held it up for him to see. "What do you think?"

"It's a dress."

"Right."

"It's not white."

"Wedding dresses aren't always white."

"Since when?"

Males can be so dense.

I dragged Addie to the store to try it on.

"Buy it, Addie. You can't get married in your apron."

She bought it and on the day of the wedding was running around in the kitchen in that rose-colored dress with a big white apron tied around her, screaming at everyone that the whole meal was going to be awful, wearing a very big smile. When she got to the church, she forgot to take the apron off and Flo ran to her and set things right.

At the close of the ceremony, Pastor Hall said an extra long prayer for Addie as first lady.

We all knew it was going to be a rough ride.

It was a whirlwind thirty-six-hour honeymoon back and forth to Milwaukee, where Addie said the food at the hotel was "passable, if you were close to starvation." She and G.T. stood in the entrance to the Welcome Stairways smiling at the white helium balloons that Flo and Yuri had decorated the place with.

"Happy life!" Yuri cried.

Addie gave herself a full fifteen seconds of back-home celebration and then marched into the kitchen and told Braverman that she'd thought of a new veal shank recipe that would get the locals going.

Only Addie would think about veal shanks on her honeymoon.

G.T. had been thinking, too. "Hope, I was wondering if you'd consider letting me adopt you, because I'd like more than just about anything to do this father thing officially."

You could have knocked me over.

Then he said he wondered how the best way to start with all of that was, and I smiled really big, because I didn't have to sit there like a dumb cluck.

I piled all my scrapbooks on the desk in the back office in chronological order. My heart was beating so hard and happy I could hardly stand it.

"These are all my significant life moments, G.T. You want the in-depth tour or the Cliffs Notes version?"

He sat in a chair. "I don't want to miss a thing."

That's *exactly* what a father should say.

I took out the baby animal book that showed my and Addie's life together reinforced through the animal kingdom. I showed him all my report cards and the photos of all the schools I'd attended. I showed him my thoughts on food service in three time zones. I showed him all the menus from all the places Addie worked at. I showed him a piece from my cast when I broke my leg in fifth grade; I showed him the first dollar I'd ever gotten as a waitress, plasticized right there by the picture of me standing at the counter of the Rainbow Diner with Spiro, the owner, doing his Greek dance by the decaf urn.

"I've been keeping these for my real father, who I've never met, G.T. But you're as real and true a father as a human being will get in this world."

He grinned so big. "That's the nicest thing anyone ever said to me."

I showed him my mother's Christmas letters. He put his hand over my hand when I told him about Deena. I showed him my savings account book with all the money I'd saved for college. It took a while to get through the scrapbooks because you can't just rush through a life. I decided not to tell him about Gleason Beal—passed over the letter I wrote to Gleason before we left Brooklyn. I didn't want to sound stupid.

He listened and listened and when I was through he said, "I am so glad you did this for me."

All along I was keeping these for G.T., I just didn't know it.

Then G.T. got up and walked over to two little trees that were growing in pots under special lights in the corner by the window. They were a wedding gift from Pastor Hall. G.T. was going to plant them out back in the spring. He lugged them over to where I was standing, knelt down, took out his Swiss Army knife and sliced a branch off one tree; he sliced a bit off the other tree. Then he held the cut branch over the other tree's cut part.

What was he doing?

"Get me that twine, Hope, over there on the table. Get the scissors, too, and that tape."

I got everything.

"Hold this branch on there with your hand."

I held it as he cut a piece of tape, cut a piece of string, and taped that small branch to the other tree, cut parts touching. He tied it with twine to make it sure.

He stood up, put the tree back under the grow light. "There. That's what's going to happen to us. It's called grafting. Taking something from one place and fixing it to another until they grow together. We didn't start from the same tree, but we're going to grow together like we did. You watch it in the next month or so and you'll see."

I don't think there was a better thing a father could have done.

I watched that plant in the office every day.

Watered it; misted it. I loved thinking about it like G.T. said, but part of me was worried the tree surgery wouldn't take. Something would go wrong and then I'd be stuck with a metaphor that couldn't go the distance.

"Don't kill it with fretting," G.T. said.

February hit hard; I felt like I was in Alaska. Snow two feet deep; wind chill put life in the deep freeze. But slowly, surely those two branches knit together, and when a month was up, G.T. pulled the bandage off and said, "There. That's us now."

I stared at the branch that had grown into the other tree. Here all along I'd thought I was going to get a father in a completely different way. But that's the lesson of the Welcome Stairways—you don't know which way a thing will come at you, but you need to welcome it with your whole heart whichever way it arrives.

The best thing about having G.T. as an official grafted father was that he lived each day to the full.

The worst part was that we didn't know if he would stay in remission.

Leukemia can come back, the doctors warned. You live with that.

Addie helped me deal with the uncertainty. "We're going to get as much as we can with the time we've been given. We're going to be grateful for whatever time that is."

I was used to living with unsureness, but it's so hard when you love someone so much and you want them always to be there no matter what.

It made the days extra special somehow—everything we did was heightened. Every day after school G.T. would ask me, "What's the best thing that happened today?" Some days were completely without meaning, but it got me thinking about the little surprises the days hold that sometimes we pass over.

It's a complete rush to get what you've been hoping for— to get it so full and complete that it fills your senses. I'm not saying it was perfect. I'd lived all my life having to contend with only one full-time adult, and now I had two stubborn ones trying to steer my life and they were getting used to *each other* in the process. We were also trying to merge two apartments and make them one. G.T. put in a door connecting the adjoining walls, but Addie thought the door looked out of place. G.T. mentioned that it was too late to change it now. They both looked at me.

I backed out of the room.

I wasn't walking through that minefield.

Last week I looked up the word *father* in my dictionary. Here's the definition: *A man who has begotten a child.*

But I think Mr. Webster didn't get it quite right.

A father isn't just woven from strands of DNA. A true father is dedicated and unshakably there for his kid every single day.

So, if you ask me what it's like to have G. T. Stoop as my father, I'll tell you: It's like having a huge tree sprout up almost overnight on your lawn. Even though it showed up quick, the steadfastness of it is going to last through the storms and the winds and the seasons.

G.T. was making a real difference in Mulhoney, too.

He began in several places all at once.

Opened the tax assessor's office.

Appointed Adam Pulver head of Students for Community Involvement—an action group that looked at the problems in the town and determined how teenagers could help make things better.

Appointed Mrs. Pettibone to head up a committee to plan a geriatric wellness center that would improve the quality of people's lives.

We had town meetings and people left not hating each other.

Brenda Babcock had slapped another stiff fine on the Real

Fresh Dairy for disturbing the peace with their big bruiser milk trucks. She had investigations going round the clock on Eli Millstone's financial schemes, too. She was redefining honor and professionalism in the sheriff's office.

As the days went by, the Real Fresh Dairy paid their back taxes and G.T. used that money to help the schools, repair the community center, and fund programs for the poor.

"What's the best we can be?" G.T. asked an assembly of teenagers, me included. And together we came up with a plan to do volunteer work for people who were short on cash.

We helped at the expanded day care facility. Anastasia was there now, learning to eat with a spoon. She'd hurl applesauce in our faces and start laughing.

We manned the Gospel of Grace's new twenty-four hour family shelter. Braverman and I tried to work there on Friday nights.

We fixed fences, mowed grass, and painted houses. We were only okay house painters. Jillian said it was good we weren't charging.

But we kept trying.

And we learned that you don't have to be famous or rich or physically healthy to be a leader. You just have to try to be a true person. We learned that helping other people brings out the good in everybody.

G.T. had figured out the big concept in government. "Politics," he kept telling us, "isn't about power, control, or manipulation. It's about serving up your very best."

I love the fact that it took a short-order cook to get it right.

20

The summer I graduated, G.T. started slipping.

Two years from when Addie and I had arrived in town.

One and a half years since he had become mayor.

I'd been accepted at Michigan State for the fall term. Squeezed in with my grades. Wowed them with my personal essay on life and food service. Braverman finally was going to college with help from a town scholarship G.T. had set up. Combined with the money he and his mother had been saving, it was just enough. The University of Wisconsin was the lucky place.

I was going to miss him like crazy.

In early July, the leukemia came back at G.T. with a vengeance, like a huge wind toppling a small boat.

The doctor said it was doubtful he could pull out of this one.

I told myself it wasn't true.

The thing that had been stalking us from behind was now in front.

My father was dying.

Addie sat with him round the clock except when I relieved her, which I tried to do often. I couldn't seem to sit in the room with him as long as she could. I needed to go outside, feel life on my face, feel winds of healing.

Braverman seemed ever-present—a huge tree himself; someone to hold on to. He was broken at the prospect of losing G.T.

For four awful weeks we watched him slip a little more each day.

I didn't think I was strong enough to handle this.

I couldn't stand the thought of this loss.

I was sick of life being so impossibly hard.

I started sitting with him for longer stretches. When I had to cry, I'd leave the room. But one day he said to me, "I don't mind if you cry, Hope."

Well, I lost it full right there. And I said something I hadn't planned.

"G.T., I need to read you something."

I sat on his bed and showed him the letter I'd written to Gleason Beal after he took our money. I couldn't mail it, of course, since he'd skipped town. I'd sealed it up in an envelope and on the outside I'd written, *To be read at another time.*

I opened the envelope slowly and remembered crying so hard when I was writing it, saw some of the tear-stained ink on the paper. I read the first line, "To Gleason Beal, who I once trusted." I stopped, looked at G.T.

"Go ahead."

Big breath. "I think I want to change my name back from

Hope to something else because what has happened has made me not believe in things to hope for like I once did. Gleason, I want you to know that I hate you for taking our money, but mostly I hate you for pretending to be a different person than you were. You stole from everyone who trusted you here.

"You took Addie's savings and her dream. You took my trust and I believed that you were my friend, but I will never be dumb enough to do that again.

"You took Charlene away from her husband because you got her to run away with you.

"You did all of it for money, but I want you to know something. I never want money to be that important to me that I would hurt someone else. I don't believe that down deep you'll ever enjoy that money just like I don't believe that people who lie or cheat or get away with things really enjoy themselves because there's a price to pay in this world. You can have the money, Gleason, but I've decided you can't have my name. I don't know how long it's going to take, but I'm going to get the feelings back about being hopeful again. I don't have them now, but I'm going to get them again. I hope you get caught and thrown in jail. When I find my father ..."

I couldn't read anymore.

"Go ahead," G.T. said. "Finish it."

I was crying good now. "When I find my father I know he's going to do something to get you what you deserve." I looked at G.T. "That's all I wrote."

He looked pretty gray but he asked me, "How do you feel about that now?"

"I feel stupid about it."

"Why?"

I shrugged.

"Is it because you wrote the part about your father coming to give him what he deserves and I'm not looking much like I can do that for you?"

Now I felt so bad I'd bothered him with this.

"Tell you what," he said. "If you stick that anger behind you, one day you're going to turn around and find it's gone."

"I'll try."

He smiled at me with such promise; I felt at that moment he was going to rise up from the bed all well, but he didn't.

"I've got to tell you selfishly, Hope, if Gleason Beal hadn't done what he did, you and Addie wouldn't have come up here and I can't imagine what my life would have been like without the two of you."

I took his hand; it felt cold.

I was crying so bad I couldn't say anything, just squeeze his big cold hand.

He died the next day.

Addie was with him. I was in my room getting dressed. But somehow I knew.

I closed my eyes; felt in my heart a brush of angels' wings, and sensed those angels coming up the welcome stairways, one from the left and one from the right, to guide G.T.'s spirit on the flight up to heaven.

21

I will never forget the flowers.

Mounds of them everywhere in heaps and piles circling the diner, lining the welcome stairways. Notes plastered on momentary cardboard frames telling of how much G.T. meant to people.

Adam's: *I don't understand why we lost you so soon when we still need you so much.*

That's the question. The worst kind, too. There isn't an answer.

The loss rolled over me like waves.

I moved in a blur of strength and sadness.

Addie closed the diner.

She had a right.

It sat there darkened like a shut-up tomb, lifeless without G.T. walking through it.

We should board up the windows, I thought. Batten down the hatches. This storm has taken too much.

But Mrs. Pettibone came with vases and vases of flowers.

"Put them inside," she said. "Turn on the lights. Let people see."

And we did. Lined the counter with them three deep, put some of the flowers from outside in water glasses, clustered them on the tables. Braverman brought his candle from the kitchen and lit it; we got more candles and lit those, too. I got the prism Harrison gave me, put it by the cash register. As the sunlight hit it, dozens of rainbows appeared on the walls.

People stood on the porch pressing their faces against the windows to see the memorial to the man we all loved.

Braverman held on to me, I held on to him. Anchors in the storm.

Addie got through it, stiff faced, trying as best as she could to hide her broken heart.

People clogged the Gospel of Grace Evangelical Center.

Al B. Hall stood by G.T.'s open casket and declared with all his might, "G.T., my good friend, how on this earth can we thank you for the life you lived to the fullest measure? Let our memories of you stretch us every day to live with all we've got and everything we know to be true."

The Gospel of Grace choir started singing something slow and bluesy that made you sway. People walked past, touching G.T.'s folded hands for one last time.

I stood by the casket with Addie and Braverman. I don't know how long I stood there. I don't know what was going on around me. All I know is that in the midst of the biggest stabs of loss, I realized that I was the perfect daughter for him.

Everything in my life had prepared me for it.

I knew firsthand about life being hard.

And I knew about being strong.

*　*　*

In the weeks following G.T.'s funeral, I learned how memory hides in the craziest places. Some days I'd be just fine, on others I would see something—anything. A plate piled with hash browns, a man with a bald head—and the mounds of flowers would stream back again into my mind and I'd start sobbing like Bambi Barnes losing it by the decaf urn.

Then I'd pull myself together and take another order.

The sad heart needs work to do.

But through it all I held Mrs. Pettibone's words in my heart—the ones she spoke to me after the funeral when she took my hand, looked into my face and said, "You've got your father's eyes."

I was leaving for college in three days. Part of me was happy to be going, the other part never wanted to leave this place. Braverman and I decided to leave for school at the same time. Neither of us wanted to be the one left in the diner waving good-bye. Adam had already headed off to Northwestern University. Jillian had left for Purdue.

We were all going to be scattered.

I hate leaving places I love.

I was standing behind the counter getting things ready for the dinnertime crowd—filling the salt and pepper shakers, getting the good grainy mustard in the little glass jars, putting the sugar in the canister, setting places so I wouldn't have to do that when the customers showed up. Lou Ellen waved good-bye. She was going to pick up Anastasia at day care. Anastasia could say mama and bye-bye now. Lou Ellen said she was learning at her own pace and that was just fine.

I was moving in and out with the grief these days, not crying every day like I had been in the beginning.

I had a few more things to pack before I left. Addie had given me the painting of the little ship on the choppy ocean that G.T.'s mother, my grandmother, had painted. My grandmother. I loved saying that. I was going to put it right above my bed in the dorm. I was wondering about everything, like who my roommate would be, would I do well in school, what was it like to be in college?

So much had changed here. So much was the same. Brenda Babcock was appointed the acting mayor to fill out G.T.'s term by the new Town Council. She was the best choice in the world, too. Like Flo said, she'd protect all the paths G.T. had laid, but would also leave her own footprints. Eli Millstone had his share of things to explain. He was letting his big-deal lawyer do most of the talking. So far he'd managed to stay out of jail. I heard he had a talk radio show and was busy running seminars for people who wanted to get into politics.

"Lord, preserve us," cried Flo when she heard *that*.

Day after day people poured into the Welcome Stairways talking about G.T. and what he'd meant in their lives. It was a privilege to know how many people had loved my father.

I knelt down, looked under the counter for just the right place. I took out my blue marker and wrote HOPE WAS HERE in small letters right above where we kept the honey jar. I'd taken my mother's advice—a small bowl of lemon wedges sat next to the honey; I kept a large bottle of Tylenol there to refill the small one I carried in my apron in case a customer had a headache. A good waitress has to be ready for anything.

I looked at the HOPE WAS HERE, so different from the ones I had written before. This time, I was coming back. This was really home.

Then the front door of the diner opened. A sea of people filled the window booths. More came in, sat at the counter.

I look at Flo and grin.

We're in the weeds.

"Look sharp now," Addie shouts from the kitchen.

Michael, our new busboy, rushes with menus and setups. Yuri, now a waiter, bows to the two women at the corner table.

"I am pleased to serve you tonight."

Those women grin so bright.

Flo's running past me saying we'll split the window booths. More people crowd the tables. A bus must have pulled in.

I'm cutting a wide berth around Yuri—he tends to veer left before he makes a right turn like a bad driver.

"I shall now bring to you the coffee, ladies. This is all right?"

I'm at the six-top near the window. Everyone has ordered except the big man in the yellow shirt. He looks tenderly at Addie's chicken pot pie special and sighs deep.

"I haven't had chicken pot pie since my grandmother made it. Is it really good here?"

I lift both hands like, *Are you kidding me?* And right there two people from different backgrounds and generations find connection in this crazy world.

That's the power of comfort food at work.

I'm at the galley calling in orders. Braverman and Addie are moving like machines. I'm back to the first day I saw G.T. flipping eggs.

Come get this miracle breakfast, Florence, before I eat it myself.

Braverman raises an eyebrow, throws his spatula and catches it behind his back. Addie smiles at me. I grin back.

I'm rushing back and forth with coffee, tea.

Sweeping through the counter, getting orders. Adrenaline pumping. If you want a thrill there's nothing like in-the-weeds waitressing. You never know what's coming next. You could wait on a maniac or a guy passing out twenties.

I deliver buttermilk fried chicken with biscuits and warmed chunky applesauce to the couple on table five. The man grabs a drumstick, takes a bite and says, "Ohhhhh. I'm in heaven."

I grin. "That's what we aim for here."

I hear the two dings.

Going to miss that sound.

I run to the galley. Joy and sadness mix together like cream in coffee.

People say it's so awful that I only had a real father for less than two years and then had to lose him.

I wish like anything he was still here, but it's like getting an extraordinary meal after you've been eating junk food for a long time. The taste just sweeps through your sensibilities, bringing all-out contentment, and the sheer goodness of it makes up for every bad meal you've ever had.

Literature Circle Questions

USE THESE QUESTIONS AND ACTIVITIES THAT FOLLOW TO GET MORE OUT OF THE EXPERIENCE OF READING *HOPE WAS HERE* BY JOAN BAUER.

1. Why do Addie and Hope leave Brooklyn? Describe what happens at their former job that forces them to look for other work.

2. Why is Hope so reluctant, at first, to spend more time with Braverman?

3. Explain the scandal that forces Millstone to resign as Mulhoney mayor and allows G.T. to take over.

4. Discuss the reasons Hope takes up boxing and then suddenly decides to give it up.

5. The big Real Fresh Dairy employs most citizens in Mulhoney. However, a lot of the people in town don't like the fact that the plant is there at all. Why not? Why are some of them scared to criticize the Dairy?

6. Why does Hope wear the clown nose in the restaurant while her mother is visiting?

7. At the beginning of the book, Hope is reluctant to leave Brooklyn — where she is comfortable and has good friends — to come to a strange, small town in Wisconsin. Describe a time you had to enter a new, unfamiliar situation, such as a new grade, school, or even a new town.

8. Hope fantasizes about meeting her father and wonders what she would say to him if they did meet. If you could meet anyone in the world, who would it be? What would you say if you saw them randomly, while walking down the street?

9. Writing seems to be very important to Hope — she writes poems, keeps a diary, and writes letters, even ones she doesn't send. Explain why you think writing is so important to her. When you write about an event, what does the act of writing compel you to do?

Note: These literature circle questions are keyed to Bloom's Taxonomy: Knowledge: 1-3; Comprehension: 4-5; Application: 6-7; Analysis: 8-10; Synthesis: 11-12; Evaluation: 13-14.

10. Even though G.T. eventually adopts Hope, in what ways does he act like a father to her long before that?

11. Describe Hope's relationship with her mother. Does her attitude toward her mother change throughout the story? Show examples of the good things her mother does for her, as well as the things that frustrate Hope.

12. Toward the end of the book, G.T. and Hope cut a branch from one tree and graft it onto another, allowing the two to merge and grow together as one. How is this natural process symbolic of the way that Hope's life has merged with the friends she's made in Mulhoney?

13. What kind of candidate do you think G.T. was? What kind of ideas did he have, and how did they differ from his opponent's?

14. Explain why Hope is a more fitting name than Tulip. Summarize the ways in which Hope tries to live up to her name.

Activities

1. Pick a vivid passage from the book that stands out in your mind. Then, draw a picture of that scene with markers or other materials — making sure to use lots of color. Next, show the picture to a friend and ask them to describe what they see. How is what they describe different from what actually happened in the book?

2. Delicious, homemade food can lift someone's spirits, make them feel better — just as it does at the Welcome Stairways Diner. Perhaps that's why it's called "comfort food." Is there a favorite meal that always makes you feel better? Make a menu of some of your favorite foods, and describe whether that food has any special healing powers.

3. Write a letter to someone you see and talk to every day, someone who's very important to you. Tell them why you're thankful they are a part of your life. Try to describe feelings and emotions that wouldn't normally come up in conversation, or point out good qualities of theirs that you might often take for granted. You don't have to send it, but you may want to.